The Troynt In The Circle

Written and Illustrated

by

A. Wales

𝔄𝔚some 𝔅ooks

First published in Great Britain in 2001 by
AWsome Books, 1 Wide Lane Close, Brockenhurst SO42 7TU

Copyright © 2001 A. Wales

ISBN 0 9539904 3 5

Printed in Great Britain by El Alamein Press Ltd, Salisbury

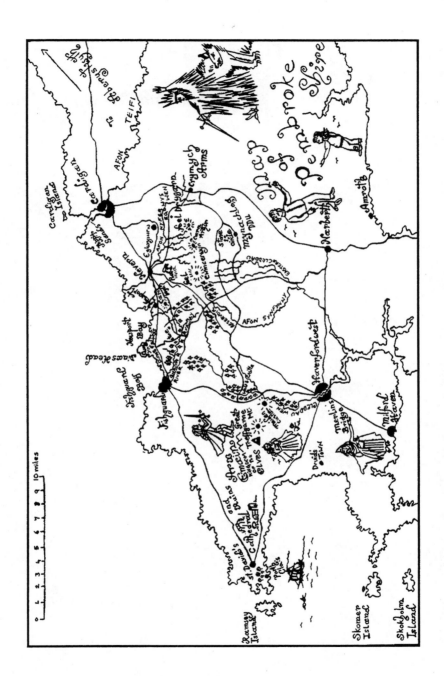

THE TRILOGY

The Troynt, The Scarab and The Goat

PART I

The Troynt In The Circle

To Aurora —
With Best Wishes
from
Ann Wales.
Happy Reading
2003!

PREFACE

The Troynt, The Scarab and The Goat

It all began with a stone from St. David's, a large volume in Ancient Welsh from Aberystwyth University, and Peter and Sarah, who have been wanting me to tell their story for at least the last thirty years. My two shadow children had been with me ever since I began writing stories at school. They came into being properly during the family holidays in Wales.

Pembrokeshire, the Prescelly Mountains in particular, is a very strange place, with ancient monuments strewn around every few yards. One can well imagine that Elves or, in Welsh, *Ellyllon*, the Family of Beauty, are never far away. I always wanted to meet them and Peter and Sarah, through the power of the miraculous stone are able to do so.

The stories are rooted in a strong family background. We first meet the children with their Aunt Myfanwy (Aunt Myf) who usually has them for the summer holidays, while the children's archaeologist parents teach at University summer schools. Peter and Sarah are taken to visit St. David's and it is there that Peter discovers a strange looking stone, it is the *Stone of Gardar*. Little does he realise that it is a long lost treasure of the Elves of Arx Emain, a stone of great power and a portal to other dimensions. It is then that the adventures really begin!

The first book of these trilogies concerns the continuing battle for Power between Gwyn-ap-Nudd, King of Arx Emain and Lord of the Elves, and Arddu, the Dark One. The ancient Stone of Gardar could be an aid to either side. Its discovery by Peter is a vital element of the struggle.

When the war between the Elves and their adversaries is over, Peter and Sarah's Mother and Father, Dr. and Mrs. Jones, are brought to Wales. They meet Anir who is a long lost relation of Peter and Sarah's Mother and their Aunt Myf. He is the Guardian of the lands around Arx Emain (the magical realm of Gwyn-ap-Nudd). He accompanies Peter and Sarah on many of their adventures in his capacity as envoy between humankind and the world of magic.

During the course of the trilogies, the whole Jones family enlarges and evolves and strengthens its bonds. As archaeologists, Mother and Father Jones are frequently busy on digs around the world, often in Classical Lands. Peter and Sarah often travel with them, enabling them to discover the ties between history, magic and mythology. Whenever ancient monsters are disturbed, they know they can rely on the Elves and their friends to help them out. As the miraculous Stone of Gardar makes time travel possible, the children meet many heroes from ancient times.

Book four sees the return of another monster from antiquity, the Troynt, or the Twrch Trwyth. This time it appears in its original form, not as the boar chased by King Arthur. This adventure begins in Cornwall, with Peter and Sarah staying with their cousins Emma and Amy, Aunt Louise and Uncle Giles. Strange goings-on at a stone circle, involving The Sympathetic Earth Movement, lead to even odder happenings in the Welsh Mountains! The Elves are forced to come to the rescue in due course.

Book five returns to Greece. Well, Cassandra DID say to Peter and Sarah that they would, and we must not disappoint her! Once again, Merlin becomes involved, as the children search for a magic amulet that will cure the Elves of a mystery plague. The Scarab in The Kiosk is only to be discovered in the Egypt of the

Roman Empire, so the powers of The Gardar Stone must be called for once again.

Book six, The Goat Ship, begins with a very special family celebration in Scotland. It is the Golden Wedding of Great Aunt Fiona and Great Uncle Ian. Dr. Jones' archaeological interests dig up yet more monsters from the past when he visits a Viking Long Ship, with Peter, Sarah and their cousins. The Viking god Thor appears to them, seeking revenge! Anir, The Guardian, must assist Peter and Sarah in fighting him off.

Whatever does happen in the following books, the Jones family will find it interesting, exciting and exhilarating, and I am sure that my young readers will again find it gripping, entertaining and enjoyable!

CHAPTER ONE

A Holiday In Cornwall

"It's not fair!" mumbled Sarah as she cycled home from the village shop at Cwm-yr-Eglwys.

"It's not fair!"

She had had a BAD day.

A bad day at school and now, seemingly, a bad day at home. For one thing, Peter had not been at school with her today. He was not ill, or away at the dentist, or missing school for any of the other ordinary reasons. The fact was; most of Peter's class were away today. They were all visiting their secondary schools. Poor Sarah had felt quite bereft. It would be a whole two years before she was due to leave Junior School. She did not quite know yet how to cope at school without Peter by her side: at break time, at lunchtime and any other time when she needed help. How irritating it was to be without him, Sarah mused, especially today of all days.

Everything at school had been fine until second break when *Bugglitz* club happened. Bugglitz club was for children who were mad on the latest craze, which was the collecting of cards with strangely formed alien insects on them. The idea was to collect as many cards as one could, swapping the duds, or ones that were no good, for aces. Sarah had two collections at home, safely arranged in old photograph albums. The cards had been banned at school for a while, because naughty Evan Williams had been caught selling his cards for money. Some children had willingly given him their dinner money in return for aces, so eager were they to have the cards. This could not continue for long without it coming to the attention of Mrs. Jenkins, the Headteacher. She strictly forbade any cards within the portals of the school.

Sarah's cards mouldered away forlornly in their shiny black albums for at least two weeks. Mother and Father said: "Thank goodness, that's the end of that!" But they were wrong. After the second week of 'Bugglitz' famine, Mrs. Jenkins relented and the cards returned to school, but not to the playground, oh no! Mrs. Jenkins was MUCH smarter than that! A club was begun in second breaktime. Mrs. Jenkins ran the club herself and made the rules. No money was to be exchanged and cards could be swapped only during club time. No cards were allowed in the playground at other breaktimes. Each club member was required to sign a copy of the rules, or they were not able to join the club or swap their cards.

Sarah was cross this particular day, because she was interested in gaining a particularly wonderful card called Damzelle and had offered two of her classmates several aces for it. However, Katherine had promised hers to someone else and Harriet wanted to keep hers and not swap. Sarah did not want any other cards, so she had returned home with no change to the collection. Then straightaway, as soon as she had flopped onto her bed in a miserable heap, Mother called!

"Sarah, be a good girl will you; do go down to the store for me and get some lettuce and tomatoes. Then we can finish the ham off this evening. I have done some nice new potatoes and all we need is some nice salad to go with them."

"Grrrrrrr!" growled Sarah inaudibly, to Mother at least! Aloud she said:

"Coming!" and dragged herself down the stairs, out of the back door and leapt on to her bicycle once more.

It was definitely all Peter's fault. Sarah thought about it all the way to the village shop and back again.

If Peter had been at school, Sarah was quite sure that he would have magically persuaded someone to part with their Damzelle for her ace, Bugletta. He also would have been at dinner to help her, when 'Big Jim' Griffiths had elbowed her, and several other pupils, out of the queue for chips! Peter would also have known how to translate the Welsh poem that Miss Rheece wanted her class to work on that afternoon. Yes, it was all his fault that everything had gone wrong, and going shopping for Mother was just the tin lid on it all!

Sarah grudgingly parked her bicycle outside the back door and swing into the kitchen with her parcels: two lettuces that had probably seen better days and a pack of cherry tomatoes. With the greatest of luck, Sarah had also managed to purchase a *reduced* pot of coleslaw (fifty pence instead of one Pound!) and half a cucumber.

"Good girl!" Mother smiled, pleased at Sarah's additions to her list. "Well done! We shall have a feast. Grate some cheese for me will you, there's a dear. I am just going to make some lovely fruit salad for dessert."

Sarah scowled at having to grate the cheese, but did the scowling when Mother turned her back. In vain she tried to explain her frustration at doing badly with the Bugglitz cards, but Mother was unsympathetic.

"Complete waste of money the whole thing. I don't agree with any of it and I am most surprised that Mrs. Jenkins has allowed you all to have a club at all. I wouldn't! Oh Sarah, do look what you're doing. The cheese is going all over the floor. No, I don't know when Father and Peter will be back exactly, but I hope it will be soon. I am going to cook the potatoes now."

Mother busied herself round the stove and Sarah, having cleared the cheese from the floor, went to lay the table. Then she left Mother listening to a soothing piece of Mozart on the radio and disappeared into the garden. Sarah wanted to have a look at the sea while she waited for Peter. Usually it was only Father they waited for, because he often worked late at the University. Now Peter was late too!

Sarah looked into the distant waves and wondered if a distant grey blob were a seal. What would happen in the autumn when Peter moved up to the BIG school in Cardigan? He would go early with Father, who would deliver him to school in the morning. Then Peter would come home on the bus, which meant he might be late every day. The school bus was notable for taking *for ever* as it dropped all the children off all over the place. A black cloud settled, almost visibly, over Sarah's head. It had a large label on it marked MISERY.

Half an hour passed. Supper must be ready by now. Suddenly, Sarah heard Mother ringing the supper bell from out of the back door. She ran back to the house. Father and Peter were already settled at table. Peter was helping himself to the lettuce, which had crisped up nicely.

"All together again. This is good!" said Father.

"Hi, Sis!" said Peter, his face still flushed with the excitement of his day. "How did you get on without me?"

"OK, I suppose," muttered Sarah, as she took some of the ham.

Then Peter, unprompted, launched into a description of what his new school was like. Everything was marvellous, apparently! The teachers were great, the uniform was *cool,* the facilities for sport were unparalleled and the classrooms were full of fascination. Sarah listened and the invisible black cloud over her head grew and grew, until by the end of the meal she was hardly polite. Peter was in full flow about how great school dinners and snacks were.

"You can even have pizza at breaktime," he announced.

Having forgotten completely that in only two year's time, she too would have the benefit of pizza at break, Sarah got up from the table and stomped off in a huff.

"Hey, what's wrong?" asked Father, "you didn't ask to leave the table."

"Sorry," muttered Sarah, "got a headache!" she said by way of an excuse.

Then she went upstairs and shut herself in her room.

"She's had a bad day, poor girl," Mother said, as she cleared the table.

"Well, I'm sorry she has gone," Father said, "because there is something I wanted to tell you all."

"Oh?" said Peter and Mother together.

"Yes, family conference," Father put on his *serious* face, "it concerns the Easter holidays, which will be with us shortly."

"What about the holidays, dear?" Mother asked.

"It's like this;" continued Father, frowning slightly, "the University want me to attend the next Meeting of the Panel of International Archaeologists."

"Great," said Peter, "are we all going too?"

"I'm afraid you can't this time," said Dr. Jones, noting the sudden disappointment spreading over Peter's face. "I can only take Mother, and you will have to come my dear, I just couldn't possibly do without my secretary. Peter and Sarah will have to stay with someone. The Meeting does not provide for any of the delegates bringing children, and we could not afford to fund them just now anyway."

"Very well dear. But what ARE we to do about Peter and Sarah? What are they to do? It so happens that I know Aunt Myf cannot have them for the first part of the holidays anyway. She, Tomos and Catrin are off to some kind of Policeman's conference in Blackpool."

"Yes, I know that, but she could have them the following week. I was wondering if during the first week Aunt Louise might put them up in Falmouth. After all dearest, you did have Emma and Amy to stay last summer when she wasn't well."

"Yes I did," said Mother thoughtfully. "Hmmm! That is a possibility. What do you think Peter?"

Peter's elation over the new school had swiftly evaporated out of the window. This was not at all what he wanted. Emma and Amy were OK, for GIRLS, but they had a nasty tendency to disagree with each other. They had nearly come to blows several times last summer. Would they prove better or worse on their own territory?

"I think I'd like to sleep on it," Peter said, as he too left the table.

"Fine, but don't forget to tell Sarah about the plans. I shall want an answer by tomorrow afternoon at the very latest."

"Yes Dad, I'll tell her. I think I shall turn in myself now. It's been a busy day."

With that, Peter disappeared up the stairs leaving Father and Mother to discuss the plans further.

Sarah was lying face down on her bed. Peter knocked on her door and entered as soon as he heard a muffled:

"Cub id."

He went straight to stand by the bedroom window and looked out into the garden. This way he would not notice, on purpose, that Sarah had been crying. Peter wondered how to break the news of their unexpectedly busy holiday to her. Outside, mist and cloud hung over the sea as it began to rain.

Sarah sat up and wiped her eyes with her fists.

"Well, how was it really?" she asked.

"What?" Peter remained at the window.

"Your day, silly, the new school!"

"Oh that."

"You don't sound as thrilled about it as you did downstairs."

"Oh I was and I am; but something happened just now that rather takes the shine off it all! I am feeling rather like a bottle of lemonade that has gone quite flat."

Sarah was curious:

"Why, what has happened to make you feel like that? I thought it was only me that was having a bad day!"

Peter turned the conversation round on her:

"Did you have a bad day, Sis?"

"Rotten! I didn't get any aces at the club today. Then I wanted you to help with the Welsh lesson that we had this afternoon and that awful 'Big Jim' Griffiths pushed me and half the class out of line at dinners."

"Oh!" said Peter, "that bad, Eh!"

"And as soon as I got home, I had to go shopping in the village for Mum. What's your *beef*? You liked your new school didn't you?"

"Oh I did. It was OK. That has nothing to do with why I'm feeling flat."

"Well what then?"

"Only that it looks as if we might have to spend half our Easter hols. in Falmouth with our *dear* cousins!"

Peter held his head in his hands in mock horror. To his surprise, Sarah leapt off the bed and danced round her room with every sign of being highly delighted.

"Oh great, really? Your not just putting me on, are you Peter? Say it's not a joke."

"I might have expected that you'd like the idea," Peter said.

"Why have we got to go?"

"Because Mum and Dad have to go to some boring old Archaeology conference and no one else can have us, that's why!"

"But where do we go for the second week?"

"Aunt Myf I think, hang on, I think I can hear Mum coming up the stairs."

He was right. Shortly afterwards, Mother came into Sarah's room and sat down on the bed. Her two children looked expectantly at her.

"Ooh Mummy, when are you going to ask Aunt Louise if we can stay with Emma and Amy?" asked Sarah eagerly, bouncing up and down on her bed.

All the problems of her day were forgotten.

"Just calm down, please dear, and don't bounce on your bed like that; it will ruin the springs."

"But when?"

"I have already telephoned to Aunt Louise. She is quite happy for you both to stay in Falmouth for the first week of the holidays. I shall take you down there by car on Sunday and Aunt

Myf will collect you from there, probably on the Saturday following. Your Father and I have to leave for the conference early on Monday."

"Where is it?" asked Peter.

"In Spain, Granada, I think. Father is very interested in the Moorish excavations that they have been doing in Spain recently. I must say, it all sounds absolutely fascinating and I expect we shall be going to look at some of them while we are there."

"Why couldn't we go?" asked Sarah, a little wistfully.

"Because, my sweetheart, the conference is for grown-up archaeologists and not for little girls, or boys either," she added, looking at Peter.

"Well, if I have to go, I have to go," said Peter, "but I'd much rather go and stay with Ben."

Ben was Peter's best friend.

"I'm sorry darling, that isn't possible, I can't have one of you going one way and the other going another way. Anyway, I am quite sure that Aunt Louise and Uncle Giles will give you a good time. Then Aunt Myf and Uncle Tomos will have you for the second week and you always have a good time with them. Father and I will be back in good time to see you back to school. Now be good dears and get some rest. Your Father and I have much to discuss and to sort out. We shall come along to say goodnight to you shortly."

"All right, Mum," said Peter, "we'll have our baths and get ready, won't we Sarah."

"Absolutely!"

"Very well then, but don't be long. See you soon."

Mother got up from the bed and left them to it.

"That is a *fait accompli*, then," said Peter.

"A what, what?"

"A *fait accompli*; I think it means that everything was sorted out before we had time to think it over. It's French you know.

Come on, though Sarah, you have first bath. I'll run the water for you while you clean your teeth. Perhaps that will make up for some of your rotten day."

"Thanks Peter, run the water nice and deep. If I have a bit of a soak, I'm sure I'll sleep well tonight."

But Sarah was wrong. After Mother and Father had been to say goodnight, Sarah found that she could not get off to sleep whatever she did. First she lay on her left side, then she lay on her right side. Then she lay on her back. Then she repeated the whole sequence until it became rather like a figure in some kind of strange dance. Eventually, when Sarah did fall asleep, she remained restless and was troubled with dreams. Just before she woke up the next morning, Sarah experienced a dream that was very clear and quite frightening.

Sarah felt herself to be walking, although she could see nothing. Then, around her, mists swirled, birds cried and something told her that she was near the sea. Next, Sarah found herself standing on the top of a rocky cliff, very, very high up. She felt frightened; not because she was at the top of the cliff but because there was DANGER in the air! Sarah felt she was waiting, waiting for she knew not what. IT was coming! She knew; at any minute IT would come. Waves broke loudly on the shore, far below her. She felt her tongue cleave to the roof of her mouth. A huge ripple appeared on the surface of the waters. Sarah knew it was a THING of total terror. Its fearful head broke through the waves... then she woke up, because Peter was shaking her.

"I say Sarah, I can hear you snoring in my room. Turn it down a bit will you, a chap can't get a decent lie in with that row going on!"

"I was dreaming, sort of. I think it was a nightmare."

"Well, you certainly gave a loud squeak just now. That's why I came in to see what was up with you."

"I'm all right now thanks, brother mine. It was the oddest dream though."

"You had better tell me while we get washed. Your clock says it's time to get ready for school."

So Sarah told him all about it. Peter said that he was sure it must mean something and Sarah said that, yes, it probably meant that they should keep away from very tall cliffs when they got to Falmouth! Peter agreed, but only in part. He found himself wondering over lunch, which was tuna, sweetcorn and mayonnaise sandwiches, whether there was not more to it. What sort of monster would arise from the waves like that? He went to see Sarah about it during the lunchtime break.

"Can't remember. I don't think I saw it properly. All I know is that it looked a very odd shape, not right at all, like nothing I have ever seen before."

"Is that all? You didn't get a glimpse?"

"Only out of the corner of my eye, so to speak, all I can tell you is that it had a beak. Now look Peter, I'm sorry but I've simply got to go. Sophie has promised to swap a Buglit for a Buglette."

"Oh, those stupid cards again! I'm glad I didn't get too interested in them."

"You did to begin with."

"No I didn't."

"Yes you did."

"No I didn't."

"Sorry Peter, here's Sophie. Gotta go! Bye! And yes you did!"

Irritatingly, Sarah had had the last word, and flew off with her friend before Peter could retaliate. He went to sit in a quiet place to think. As was usual in such circumstances, he took himself away to the infant's garden, which had a seat. It was unusual for Sarah to have dreams like that, he thought.

A Monster from the sea... the thought of it somehow gave him a *bad* feeling in the pit of his stomach. However, it was only a dream and probably not worth contacting Anir, who was their friendly go-between and guide to the Kingdom of the Elves. He was The Guardian of Arx Emain, a very special and important person indeed.

Thinking about things, Peter cast his mind back to the last occasion that he and Sarah had seen Anir. Anir was Peter's special and most particular Hero, so he was always very glad to see him. They had come upon him down by the rocks near their very own private beach. He was sitting and watching the seals play and appeared not to hear the children come. Peter and Sarah had crept up and quietly sat down beside him. They had all three sat silently together, watching the seals.

Then, without turning round to look at them, Anir began to give Peter and Sarah news of their Elvish friends in Gwyn-ap-Nudd's magic realm. Apparently, all was well. Peter and Sarah were interested to hear that Dylan, Anir's infant son, could talk quite well now. Already he could sing several of the Elvish songs, taught him by his mother Aneryn, from beginning to end, without making any mistakes. Sarah was eager to see him again.

"Won't you bring him over here to see us?"

"Not yet, Sarah, Aneryn does not like him to be too far from Arx Emain as yet. Anyway, I am afraid that his Welsh is bad and his English is even worse!"

"Don't you speak to him in English, Anir?" Peter asked.

"A little, but not enough really. Aneryn wants him to learn one language properly, while he is still a baby. He will come to know the others by and by."

"And what are the Elves doing?" asked Sarah.

"Doing? Why, what they are always doing, minding their own business! Unless, of course they are called upon by others to do otherwise," smiled Anir. "No, Sarah, there is nothing exciting brewing down at Arx Emain at present. That is why I was free to come here with Ederyn today."

"Ederyn!" both children sat up, eyes wide open, "is he here too?"

"Yes, he is here. He went walking further down from here on the coastal path. He has gone to see some of the sea creatures that he knows. Every now and again some of us patrol the coast to see what there is to be seen, to question, to discover and to mark any changes. Then too, we might contact Eidyol, the Watcher of the seas. He comes seldom to Arx Emain, as he prefers to be with those he watches over. Gwyn-ap-Nudd likes to know everything that passes in his Kingdom, from the sea shore to the mountain top. Not a blade of grass can be broken or bent without his coming to know of it, they say."

"Who are *they*?" said Peter.

"The Elves of Arx Emain of course!"

"When can we come there again?" asked Peter and Sarah both at once.

"Soon I expect, but not today for Ederyn will return shortly. Then we shall both go back together to Arx Emain with our report for Gwyn."

"Do you keep an eye on us too?" Sarah asked him.

"But of course; on you two most of all!"

Peter caught a slight twitch of Anir's eye, a wink meant for him alone? Peter was a special friend of Arx Emain, or wished to be. For some time now, he had nurtured a secret desire to follow Anir into the Guardianship. Only the desire was not so secret, for of course, Gwyn-ap-Nudd, Ederyn and Anir knew all about it!

"Oh see!" Sarah said.

"Now then," Anir looked up, "here comes Ederyn down the path. We must say farewell for the present. Remember, if you need us ever, there are ways and means of calling us. You both know that after all this time, you are almost regular visitors!"

Sarah and Peter greeted Ederyn. They had a special fondness for him, as he had been the very first Elf that they ever encountered. How many years ago was it? Sarah tried to think. To long ago to count, and anyway, they had had far too many adventures in between. Peter and Sarah were quite accustomed to the Elves, and Anir The Guardian, drifting in and out of their lives at irregular intervals. They were, indeed, quite phlegmatic about it.

After a short conversation, Ederyn and Anir had left for Arx Emain and Peter and Sarah had gone home for tea. Nothing, as far as they could see, was out of the ordinary. That beach encounter had been about three weeks ago. Peter jumped up suddenly as the school bell rang for the end of break and put an end to his brooding. Afternoon school threatened to displace Elves in Peter's thoughts. Even so, the monster from the sea refused to be quelled. It popped up again at odd moments; during the weekly maths test, for instance!

Several days passed. Sarah seemed to have totally forgotten her nightmare but Peter began to doodle dragons surrounded by water on his exercise books. The monster might be dead as far as Sarah was concerned, but it was not lying down. For his trouble, the reward for his artistry was a detention, with extra work during the last day of term. As fate would have it, the weather was glorious, and there sat Peter in the empty classroom with two pages of long multiplication to do.

When Sarah and Peter arrived home, Peter was feeling more than grumpy, especially at the prospect of spending the first half of the holiday with two more girls. He went upstairs, shut himself up in his room and sulked, while Sarah helped Mother pack her things for Cornwall.

Saturday was miserable. Mother and Father took Peter and Sarah to Haverfordwest where they were treated to the cinema. Frankly, Peter could not see that this was in any way compensation for deserting the two of them for the whole holiday. But afterwards, they went to a specialist chocolate shop to buy Easter Eggs and got away with having two each!

Sunday morning early, Peter and Sarah waved goodbye to Father and set off with Mother on the very long drive to Falmouth. Father was spending the day collecting all his notebooks and other gear for the conference. The drive to Cornwall was not too bad as Mother kept mainly on the motorways. At five o'clock, they arrived outside Aunt Louise's house. It was a pretty cottage on the sea front; near to one of the beaches, some pretty gardens and the cliff path.

"Here we are, then!" said Mother brightly, and encouraged Peter and Sarah to get out and unload their luggage.

Aunt Louise, Uncle Giles, Emma and Amy emerged from the cottage. Peter, Sarah and Mother were greeted warmly and swept into the cottage for afternoon tea.

"Great to see you again," grinned Emma and Amy happily.

"You too and likewise," Sarah smiled back.

Peter muttered something quite inaudible.

"You're not going all the way back to Wales now, are you?" asked Aunt Louise, with some concern.

"Oh no," Mother said, putting down her empty cup, "I'm meeting John at the hotel outside the airport. Now I really must be going. Have a good time everybody."

She kissed Peter and Sarah goodbye then she jumped back into the car and drove away. A disconsolate Peter and an excited Sarah waved her off. Emma turned to them both.

"Do you want to unpack now or go and see the beach first?" she said.

CHAPTER TWO

Strange Goings-on In A Stone Circle!

"Oh we're going to have such fun!" said Amy, pulling Sarah, complete with suitcase, up the stairs.

Emma and Peter followed behind. Sarah was going to share a room with Amy and Peter would be in the guest room. Sarah unpacked with Amy and Emma's noisy assistance. Peter's unpacking was an altogether more solitary affair. The only audience was his teddy bear, the ONE that must NEVER be mentioned.

"Dahlings!" trilled Aunt Louise up the stairs, "if you are quick, you can show Peter and Sarah the beach before supper."

Emma, Amy and Sarah were down like a shot. They waited for Peter by the front door. Three minutes later he arrived, quite unconcerned. He had made up his mind, that if the week was going to filled with GIRLS and girlish things, he would play a secret game with himself in his head. He had decided to be a prisoner of war, with the girls playing the part of his enemies. They were more than Amazon-like on occasion, especially when fighting among themselves! This first visit to the beach could be *a march to the salt mines.*

"Don't be late for supper everyone, it's fish and chips," said Uncle Giles, as he let all four children out by the back door.

They ran out and through the pleasant formal gardens, then down to the sandy beach. Amy turned two summersaults on the sand. The tide was out. Sarah and Peter both noticed that the beach sloped downwards, shelving steeply, then flattened out to reveal flat sand with little wavelets and pools carved into it. Tame, meek little waves lapped at the sands' edge.

"I can't wait until tomorrow," said Sarah, "I wonder, will it be warm enough to bathe?"

"It might not be warm enough for swimming, but you can paddle," said Emma, "you'll have to save swimming for the big baths up on top of the hill."

She pointed to a large modern building above the resort.

"It's really *cool*, all my friends go there."

"What's the fort?" asked Peter.

"It's something to do with Henry the Eighth's defences for Falmouth, I think. There are loads of little forts all over the place," said Amy.

"If you want rock pools, there are zillions of them just round that corner," Emma continued.

"And the town's great for shopping," added Amy, interrupting her sister.

"AND you can go for boat rides, like the one that goes over to St. Maws, or up the river Fal, or even as far as the Helford river."

Peter felt that he was beginning to warm to Falmouth, just a little, especially at the news that sea voyages might be available as part of their holiday programme!

"Let's take them up the cliff path," suggested Amy, "we can watch the sun begin to set and then come home for supper. Want to come?" she asked the two visitors.

"Why not," said Sarah, and off they all trudged.

"It was all so very pretty, as only Cornwall can be in the spring time. All the spring flowers were blooming much earlier than at Peter and Sarah's home in Wales. Small buds opened in the hedgerows to reveal a green mist that seemed to wrap around the whole land, like a swathe of green gauze. After several minutes, the four children gained the cliff top. Panting, they stood awhile to catch their breath.

"Are we going on?" asked Peter, "where does this path lead?"

"Do you want the long answer, or the short one?" asked Amy, cheekily.

"The short answer," Sarah said firmly.

"To the next beach!" replied Amy.

"Which is full of caves!" said Emma.

"What's the long answer?" asked Peter.

"Right around Cornwall, because it's the coastal walk, ha, ha," said Emma with a sigh, for she had heard Amy's joke several times before. Amy was always very proud of her jokes and always saw to it that they were exercised regularly!

"I think we had better go home," said Emma at last, "I think I can smell those fish and chips cooking!"

"Everyone likes fish and chips, except for little me," said Amy, "I have to have sausages, 'cos I don't like fish."

Sarah shivered. Something that she saw, far out to sea, suddenly reminded her of the dream she thought she had forgotten.

"Are you alright, Sarah?" Peter asked, "if you are cold you can borrow my jacket, if you like."

"I'm not cold, thanks all the same. I'll be alright in a minute; I'll just be glad to get back to the house, that's all."

When she said this, Peter realised what she was thinking. The monster from the sea was rearing its ugly head again. Little did either of them realise how very ugly this particular monster would turn out to be.

The sun began to set and the four children made their way back for supper. A fairly jolly evening was enjoyed by all. Even Peter forgot all about being a prisoner of war and his march to the salt mines.

Next morning, all woke to a bright shiny Monday morning. The weather was absolutely perfect. Emma and Amy encouraged their visitors to walk with them down the road, along the front to where the rock pools were; zillions of them, as Emma had promised.

There, all spent a merry time slooshing from pool to pool, catching all kinds of odd beasts. There were prawns, of course, but there were also pipe fish, sand fish, flat fish, other fish strangely coloured; the names of which Emma and Amy did not know, crabs and hermit crabs. In fact, there were so many fascinating creatures that everyone was surprised when Emma suddenly announced that it was lunchtime. They trailed back, wet feet and nets drying out on the return journey past a road full of smart hotels. The sea creatures they released back into the rock pools, ready for high tide.

Both Peter and Sarah found that they had lost their appetites and found even larger ones! Lunch was: Cornish pasties, gravy and greens, followed by stewed rhubarb and custard. When all had gone, Sarah still felt as if she might have managed just a little more. Peter felt sleepy after sun, sea and sand, AND a large meal. He stretched out on the sofa in Aunt Louise's sitting room, while Emma, Amy played dominoes with Sarah.

Peter half fell asleep, then after a little while, he woke up again. The girls were engrossed with their game. Peter thought that he would read the local newspaper to pass the time until the girl's game was over. He picked the paper up, not really expecting to find anything at all interesting, but the headlines made him sit up right away. Wide awake now, he read on, the hair on the back of his neck tingling as he did so.

"FIASCO OF FESTIVAL AT STONE CICLE!" it began.

Peter gathered from the article that hordes of the 'Sympathetic Earth Movement', and others of that ilk, had gathered to celebrate the new life of spring at a stone circle that was not too far away from Falmouth. There had been a huge camp around the site, not looked upon favourably by local landowners.

"Well," thought Peter, "that's normal enough!"

But the next paragraph, which described the central ceremony, gave him a real shock.

The leaders of the movement had gathered all their people round the circle while they did some kind of weird dance within it. They had, apparently, invented all sorts of strange ceremonials which continued all evening, ending at midnight with more weird dancing. Then everyone present had been encouraged to *merge*, by embracing the stones. The leaders of the Sympathetic Earthers having been the first to undertake this act. They had then stood in the centre of the circle while the rest of their followers and hangers-on did the same.

It was then, allegedly, that they had been attacked by; goodness knows what! Leaders and followers had fled in sheer terror. Half a dozen mongrel dogs had been consumed in a fire that nobody remembered lighting! The local police had been summoned to the scene to investigate. The media had already concluded that at least half the people concerned were mad and the other half were up to no good and could be pranksters. The police were keeping their conclusions to themselves, for the moment at least.

Somehow, reading this article re-awoke Peter's shared memory of Sarah's sea monster. He wondered if he should tell her about it. Then Emma looked up from the game.

"Amy's won again!" she said, "I give in, let's stop."

Then she took a look at Peter and although she did not know him all that well, she could see at once that something was wrong.

"Hey, Peter, you look very pale, is there something wrong? Have you got indigestion or something?"

In a split second Peter decided to tell the girls what he was thinking. That old feeling in the pit of his stomach told him that once again they were about to become involved with something requiring the assistance of Gwyn-ap-Nudd and the Elves. However, for the present, it was still just a hunch. He would need help if he were to gather clues.

"Just look at this!" Peter said, pointing to the article. They were all pouring over the newspaper when Aunt Louise came into the room.

"What good children; reading the newspaper are you? How very educational. If you like, for a treat, I shall take you all in our car to Lands End tomorrow. There is an adventure park there, you know."

"Oh, thank you Marmee!" cried Emma and Amy.

"Thank you very much," echoed Peter and Sarah.

Aunt Louise then left them to their own devices, to fill the rest of the afternoon as they desired, and went to have a nap to ready herself for the exertions of the following day.

Ten minutes later the four were on the beach with the newspaper, having a pow-wow.

"Don't you see, it's perfect!" insisted Emma. "If we ask Mummy to drive via Penzance, we can fix it that we might even get to picnic right near those Stones. I think I know where they are, and I'm sure they are not too far from the road. If you really want to look at the *horror site*, we could do it. I'm sure we could!"

"I'm not actually sure that I do want..." began Sarah.

"Oh, come on, be a sport," pleaded her brother.

He began to feel a thrill. He was on the scent!

"I'm with Sarah," said Amy, "I just want to go to Lands End."

But eventually, after the discussion had gone to and fro for some time, the objectors were worn down and it was decided to see if Aunt Louise would take them via Penzance and the Stones.

"But not until we have gone to look at those caves," said Peter, "I must go and have a look at them properly."

"OK, Peter," said Emma, "but how about an ice cream first?"

"Great!" said Sarah, "whose got the pocket money?"

"We have," said Peter and Emma.

So the four of them went straight away to the beach café at the back of the sandy beach. Not only were four enormous Cornish ice creams purchased, but also fishing nets, two buckets and a spade.

"Just in case we see anything interesting on the way," as Amy said.

"Well, if the caves are no good, we can always go rock-pooling instead," said Sarah, "and we've still got Wednesday, Thursday and Friday to do that, if Aunt Louise takes us to Lands End tomorrow."

"It's really *cool* at Lands End," Amy said, "Mummy and Daddy used to take us there when we were little. There is a super adventure playground, a Pirate ship, lots of shops and places to eat. We always liked going there."

"Good, Let's hope it IS on for tomorrow then, you girls!" said Peter.

Then, getting to his feet he said:

"OK, I've finished my ice cream now. Which way do we go from here? Over the cliff path? Right, lead on, Emma and Amy. Sarah and I will follow you and I can carry most of the luggage."

"Thanks, Peter," responded Emma and Amy, "You're a PAL!"

And off they went, past the sea wall, past the beautiful gardens and up the cliff side.

"This is SO beautiful!" thought Sarah.

Even though she had a cliff walk at home; even though it was only early spring, the buds had unfurled themselves in the hedgerows and in the bushes facing the sea. Ferns had begun to show forth their minute fronds. The occasional early butterfly darted in and out of the taller grasses, looking for the spring flowers: celandines and dandelions in abundance; primroses, gorse and bluebells, enchanted the children as they passed by.

Above all, as always, Sarah adored the sight of the blue of the sea and sky, peeping through the green branches of the gorse and bramble bushes. It was pure joy and not at all a chore, to pass from the sandy beach, around the headland to the beach of the caves. When they arrived on the sands, the tide was obligingly low.

"Only we'd better not hang about," Emma said, "we don't want to be cut off by the high tide. The air-sea rescue wouldn't like it!"

They ran across the sands and climbed over the rocks on the other side of the beach. Then all at once, the caves became visible.

"I love this place," exclaimed Peter, "you have a beach for everything here: one for rock pools, one for swimming and one with caves. It's all completely perfect. Come on everyone, last ones in are Neanderthals!"

"No," corrected Sarah, "Troglodytes, we shall all be *Trogs* because we'll all be cave dwellers."

"Trogs!" said Amy, "that's a good name. I'm going to be a Trog. Do you want to be a Trog, Emma?"

"Yes, Troglodyte, you little ninny. I'm one already! Hello-o-o-oh!"

Emma's echo reverberated round the small cave into which they had all clambered. Great fun was had for several minutes, making up echoes in order to frighten off any other cave dwellers there might be in the vicinity. Amy suddenly had a thought:

"Bats!"

"What?" said the others.

"Bats, I do hope there aren't any bats in here."

Amy suddenly grabbed her sister.

"I don't like it in here any more, I want to get out!"

"All right, off you go."

"But I want you to come with me."

"But I want to stay here," said Emma, with some exasperation, "I thought you wanted to be a Trog?"

"Not now there might be bats!"

"Oh, I'm sure there aren't any," Sarah said. "Come on Amy, look, Peter is going to try digging for buried treasure in the floor here."

"I bet there's a stolen horde right under these rocks, somewhere deep beneath the sand. Help me clear away these rocks and stones, girls, and we'll soon see!"

Peter began to pull at the rocks and stones with his hands. Emma helped and after a while Amy helped too. Soon they were all taken up with the thoughts of Spanish doubloons, pieces of eight and Blackbeard's treasure. Amy wanted to know if there would be a lot of gold.

"It'll be better than winning any lottery, you'll see," said Peter.

But they did not see. There was not time enough. An hour or so later and Peter had only begun to dig the sandy floor of the cave. Emma had gone to look at the sea.

"You'll have to stop, Peter, the tide is well on its way in. Out you go, Amy. That's right Sarah. No, Peter, you really have got to stop right now!"

Emma went over to Peter, grabbed at the spade and pulled at his arm until he came. They all scrambled out of the cave, blinking slightly in the strong spring sunshine. Overhead, seagulls wheeled and turned, making their mournful cries.

"Some people say that seagulls are dead sailors turned into birds," Amy said.

"Ooooh! That's gruesome," said Sarah, looking up at the gulls.

"You've made that up," Emma remarked, "or should that be a reference to albatrosses?"

"It's true! Really it is. It's really true, Peter and Sarah, and King Arthur got turned into a Chough!"

Sarah thought that she had better change the subject.

"I think it must be time for tea by now. I could murder an iced bun and I think I saw some in your Mother's shopping this morning. Do let's go and find out."

"Yes, and I could do with a drink after all that digging. I'm parched," added Peter.

"OK, back we go then. Follow me," and Emma began to make her way over the beach towards the cliff path.

They were soon over the headland and walking past the formal gardens on their way to their cousin's cottage.

"Hello," said Aunt Louise, as they came in through the back door. "Had a good afternoon? Wash your hands everyone and then come and have some tea."

The washing of hands was completed with the greatest haste; for on the kitchen table stood a large jug of real lemonade and a plate filled with iced buns.

"Mmm! And they have cherries on top, my favourites!" Amy pronounced ecstatically.

That night, everyone turned in early. Aunt Louise said the girls must help her make sandwiches for the picnic in the morning, while Peter must do his bit by collecting up all the things deemed to be necessary for their day out. These included: the picnic rug, deck chairs, parasol, sun hats, Macs and umbrellas.

"Because you never know at this time of year WHAT the English weather is going to do!" Aunt Louise told him.

"As if I needed reminding!" thought Peter to himself.

Before they all went to bed, the four had a meeting in Emma's room. She showed them the offending Stones on their big tourist map.

"Here they are," she said, "on the B road between Newlyn, Porthcurno and Sennen."

"But we'll never get your Mum to consent to a picnic there," objected Peter, "the A road goes straight to Sennen and Lands End directly."

"Ah, but Amy and I will think of something, you'll see."

"Yes," said Amy, "it'll be something really 'neat'. We'll cook it up while we're asleep. Dreams can solve problems you know."

"I doubt it!"

"Oh, they can, Emma."

"I think it's time for sleep, all right!" Sarah said, removing herself from the rug on Emma's floor, which was a real sheepskin. "We are all going to be very busy in the morning."

They all knew that she was right, so one by one they left Emma and the map for their own beds and a good night's rest, with or without dreams.

In the morning, Sarah awoke to find Amy sitting on her bed all dressed and ready for the day. She was singing her favourite pop song.

"Am I late?" Sarah asked.

"No, it's only six o'clock, but I thought I'd get up now."

"Ugh!" with a grunt, Sarah turned over in bed and put her head under the pillow to block her ears.

Seeing that her song was not being appreciated, Amy stopped her singing and left the bedroom to go downstairs for an early breakfast.

"Thank goodness!" thought Sarah, and making herself comfortable once more, slept again. The next thing she knew, Peter was shaking her by the arm.

"Wake up, Sis! You're late. We have all had breakfast, and Emma and Amy have begun to do the sandwiches. They did not know if you would prefer egg or tuna, as well as cheese and salad."

"Oh, how delicious!" Sarah leapt out of bed feeling extremely hungry all of a sudden. "I think I'd like all three!" she cried.

"Well hurry up and dress. Then you might get all three, you greedy girl. I'm going to pack the car boot for Aunt Louise."

Peter swept out of the bedroom leaving Sarah to get herself ready as quickly as she could. When Sarah finally arrived in the kitchen, nearly all the sandwiches were done. The breakfast things were cleared away and Aunt Louise was organising the preparations for the picnic.

"Bread is in the bin and you can use the toaster. Cereal is in that cupboard under the dresser. Sugar is in the jar on that shelf above the sink and milk is on the table. I think there is some tea still in the pot," Aunt Louise directed. "Just help yourself, Sarah dear."

Sarah did so. Then when she had finished eating, she discovered that the picnic was made and all that was required of her was to help pack it in the hamper.

At ten o'clock sharp, all children, food, rugs, umbrellas, comforters and toys were in the car and ready to go. Aunt Louise locked up the house and got into the car.

"Forward troops! To Lands End we go, but not beyond!"

Everyone laughed. That was silly, for of course you cannot possibly go further than Lands End, certainly not in a car! The motor coughed and spluttered into a start. Aunt Louise drove away. A small voice from the depths said:

"But you can't go further than Lands End."

"We ALL know that," said Emma condescendingly, "Mum was making a joke."

"You're bossy!"

"No I'm not."

"Yes you are."

"Ssh! Behave yourselves, girls," said Aunt Louise, "don't fight while we have visitors or I shan't take you where you want to go. I gather you all want to take the scenic route today?"

Aunt Louise looked at Peter and Sarah , who were sitting in the back of the car. She viewed them in her driving mirror. She found herself puzzled. Why did they all suddenly want to go to picnic near stone circles? Was it something that Peter and Sarah were used to doing with their archaeologist parents? Aunt Louise supposed that it probably could not do any harm. After all, they would be there in daylight.

She had read the rather lurid account of the Sympathetic Earther's Spring Festival in the newspaper. However, she did not pay too much attention to it. The people were either out of their minds, or playing pranks, as the paper more than slightly suggested. She was mystified but decided that for today, she did not mind the detour.

It was not all that far to Penzance from Falmouth. They decided to make a stop in Penzance for elevenses and some sightseeing. Aunt Louise parked the car near the harbour. A shop selling Cornish pasties, cakes, drinks and buns soon hove into view. Ten minutes later, when cherryade and doughnuts had been consumed by all, and Aunt Louise was persuaded into adding Cornish pasties to the menu for lunch, they went to look at the ships in the harbour. After they had had a long look round, a shop selling all kinds of sea shell detained everyone for even longer. Then they walked through some very pretty gardens. Aunt looked at her watch.

"Good heavens! Back in the car, you lot, or it will be a very long time before we have lunch, and that means that we will have less time at the Theme Park."

"I could eat lunch now. Just smell those pasties. They are absolutely irresistible!"

"No Peter, hands off! Wait until we stop for lunch please. You will really want one then," said Aunt Louise.

"Anyway brother mine, you have only just finished your snack."

Peter admitted defeat. Aunt Louise walked the children back along the front to the car park. Once they were on their way, Sarah began to wonder about the Stones that they were going to see. Was it safe to picnic there? Would they find any clues as to what had attacked the 'Sympathetic Earthers'? She looked out across the sea. Every ripple seemed ominous, and a vision of her dream monster returned to haunt her. Similar thoughts played in Peter's brain, and to a lesser extent in Emma and Amy's heads too. What was the mystery of the attack at the Stones? They were possibly on the point of finding it out!

CHAPTER THREE

The Monster In The Circle

"It doesn't look very scary," Amy spoke for them all.

It was what they were all thinking. All the same, Aunt Louise having read the article about the Stones, however cursorily, decided to stay as near to the road as possible. She parked the car and spread the rugs and the picnic out as near to it as she could.

It was not the most delightful picnic site that Sarah had ever picnic'd in, but everyone did their best to enjoy themselves. The sandwiches, Cornish pasties, crisps, fruit and cola disappeared. Nearly all Aunt Louise's home made lemonade went too.

"Do leave just one bottle at least, for the return journey," begged Aunt Louise. "I'm sure you will want something to drink when you have been round Lands End all afternoon."

Reluctantly, Emma replaced the bottle she had taken out in the hamper.

"Pity," she said.

"We've not got much time to look at those Stones," said Peter, "come on you girls, I'll race you over to them."

He set off at an astonishing rate.

"Don't be too long," called Aunt Louise, "I am not waiting here all afternoon for you. The longer we stay here, the shorter the time in the Theme Park!"

This threat did not entirely fall on deaf ears. Sarah and Amy felt that they would much rather be on their way to Lands End than to these creepy Stones, with *Goodness Knows What* hanging around them.

The Stones appeared in the distance. True, they were very odd in shape, as are most of the stones that have been put into the Old Circles. Peter walked up to one of the megaliths and put his hand on it. He removed it quickly, as if he had been stung. It was as if there were some kind of electric current running through the old Stone. He felt sick.

"What's up Peter?" asked Sarah.

Her brother had gone extremely pale and all her instincts told her that something was very wrong.

"Nothing, nothing at all," he almost sounded afraid.

That was not like Peter, not the Peter she knew.

"Can you and Emma go into the centre of the circle and see if you notice anything strange."

"OK, come on Emms," and Sarah and Emma went off to investigate. Amy trailed after them, but Peter stayed well outside the Stone Circle. He watched as the girls made as thorough a search of the Circle as they could in the time allowed. They stopped in the very centre, as if they had indeed found something interesting. Then they went round once, all the way round the whole Circle, shook their heads and ran back to where Peter was standing.

"Anything?"

"Not much, just a bit of burning in the centre and off to one side of the Circle," Sarah informed him.

"And one might expect that," Emma said, "because of the description of the fried dogs in that newspaper article."

"Don't be so horrid, Emma. I'm telling Mummy of you!" and Amy ran back to the car, glad of an excuse to do so.

In spite of the bright spring sunshine, even she sensed something dark and unnatural about the place.

Peter followed Amy back at a smart pace, leaving Emma and Sarah to bring up the rear. Half way back he too began to run. Then Emma and Sarah joined in, as if it were a race.

"I won!" said Amy, when the other three turned up at the car.

They found that Aunt Louise had already packed everything away in the boot, ready to continue the journey.

"I'm ready to roll when you are," she said, "are you all done?"

"We're fine," said Emma, and they all climbed back into their seats and arranged themselves comfortably for the rest of the drive to Sennen and ultimately, Lands End.

As they drove away, Aunt Louise began to sing a *car* song. Everyone joined in. Apparently they were all feeling glad to be leaving the Stones.

"What on earth happened to you?" Sarah asked anxiously, "why didn't you want to go into the centre of the Circle?"

"Tell you later, Sarah my little sister!"

Peter was rewarded with a pinch.

"Will you please stop calling me LITTLE sister!"

"Yes, if you promise not to, OW! pinch me any more!"

"I promise," said Sarah, and then she and Peter fell silent, although Emma and Amy continued singing until they could all see the vast car parks outside the Theme Park.

"Hurray, we're here!" the four shouted loudly.

"And thank goodness for that," murmured Aunt Louise.

"When the car had been parked and the tickets had been purchased, they went down the road to see the sights.

Peter and Sarah found that Lands End was all that their cousins said it would be. Aunt Louise took them to see the cliffs and the lighthouse, a truly impressive sight.

Then followed afternoon tea in one of the restaurants, a Cornish Cream Tea, naturally! Aunt Louise then settled herself down to sit over her pot of tea for the duration of the visit, while the four children went to explore the adventure playground and pay a visit to the museum and other amusements.

They finished their afternoon in the shops, spending more of their pocket money on souvenirs.

"What have you got, Emma?" asked Amy.

"A few postcards, a nice shell and a pencil with: *Lands End* written on it."

"I've got a shell too," said Amy, "but I might give mine to Mummy."

"How sweet!" Emma remarked, looking down her nose at her little sister.

Sarah saw Red for Danger!

"Don't be like that, Emma, I think that's a very nice thought Amy," she said, and squeezed Amy's little hand. "Come on everyone, I still have loads of pocket money left. I'll buy you all an ice cream. There's just enough for a 'soft whip' each."

"With the chocolate on the top?" asked little Amy.

"Of course with the chocolate on the top," Sarah told her kindly.

"Why are we waiting?" Peter said, starting off towards the soft-ice parlour. "Come on, I can see mine melting already!"

Emma followed Peter's good example and they both ended up running for the queue. Sarah and Amy brought up the rear at a somewhat slower rate but managed to stand behind Emma anyway, who was several bodies behind Peter.

"Let those two stand in the queue," Sarah had told Amy, "I have all the money!" Amy smiled at Sarah, one of her most charming smiles.

It was while they were waiting for their part of the queue to reach the assistant in charge of serving the ice cream, that Peter gained some real information about the incident at the Stone Circle.

There was a tray of Lands End Rock to one side of the ice cream machine. A dispirited looking little family stood by it, trying to make up their minds how much of the sweet to buy. There was a man, a woman and two very tiny children. They might have been boys or girls, Peter could not immediately determine which.

The man was complaining about something or another that seemed to be disconnected with the choice of rock. As Peter was easily within earshot, he could not help overhearing what the man was saying.

"I told you we shouldn't 'a gorn to that there DO at midnight."

"Well," returned the woman, "it sounded all right on the poster, didn't it."

"Stone Hugging and Sympathetic Dancing, Huh!"

The man made a grimace.

At the mention of 'Stone Hugging', Peter's ears prickled.

He looked at the girls behind him in the queue. They were busy talking away among themselves and had not noticed this family in front of them.

"Stone Hugging," continued the man, raising his voice slightly.

He turned to face the woman, who had picked up a pink piece of rock and given it to one of her children.

"Stone Hugging," he repeated contemptuously, "they didn't have to fry my poor old Rex, now did they?"

"THEY didn't!" the woman replied.

She did not turn to look at him, but busied herself in giving another piece of rock to the other tiny child, and searching in her battered purse for some money to pay for it.

"Whatever!" the man protested, "but I think THEY started it. I think those weird friends of yours MADE that THING come to the Stone Circle."

The woman turned round to face him at last. She had paid for the sweets and the two children were sucking happily away at their rock.

"Well, I call that ridiculous," she said, "The Sympathetic Earth Movement has nothing to do with magic."

"I never said they did," argued the man, "but I say they MADE that THING come, all the same! I reckon that it came out of the water somewhere."

"What? Like the Loch Ness monster, you mean," the woman gave a sarcastic laugh, then picked up the smallest child.

Peter could see that they were about to leave and strained to hear the end of their conversation.

"Oh Kevin, you are SO stupid!" the woman said.

"It was all black and dripping with water..." said Kevin, his face suddenly contorted with horror, as he cast his memory back to the events of only a few days before. "A black shape, dripping wet, that's it, and it looked cross between a bird and who knows what!"

"I thought it looked like a horse," retorted the woman, walking towards the door of the shop.

Kevin remained where he was, as if rooted to the spot, reliving the horror of the Stones.

"It was a bird," he said, "it had a beak, though come to think of it, it did have some features of a horse. Couldn't see its hindquarters much, they were lost in some kind of strange mist. I know it had a long shaggy mane. Yes, it had a mane, but it had a beak too. It was like nothing I have ever seen before.

Then, when it got to the centre of the Stone Circle, beams of light seemed to come from the Stones themselves. It was then it bust into flames. It fried all the dogs that were in the Circle and nearly fried those fine leaders of the Sympathetic Earthers as well! Then that horrible THING came out of the Circle and just disappeared, vanished it did."

Kevin turned suddenly to the woman and shouted at her:

"I wish it had fried those blasted Sympathetic Earthers!" he cried, and putting his head in his hands, he stomped out of the ice cream parlour, past the woman and the children and off.

"WOW!" thought Peter, "Now I've heard it all, and dear Kevin has given me a full description of the THING. This is very, very interesting and very odd. I do wish that we could talk to Gwyn-ap-Nudd, or Ederyn, or Anir about it. I am sure they must know what it is."

Peter, however, was unable to wonder further on the matter. A huge cone of soft ice cream was being thrust into his face and YES, it had the chocolate on the top.

About ten minutes later, the four children had sought out Aunt Louise. She had remained in the restaurant and had taken full advantage of the capacious and overflowing tea pot.

"My mother always used to call me her little Samovar," she said with a giggle, "give me a full tea pot and I simply HAVE to drink it until it is quite empty. But come along everyone, we must be making tracks for home now, I think. It will take us an hour to get back to Falmouth from here, maybe more, depending on the traffic. That's right, Peter, you lead the way to the car park. Come along, girls, best foot forward and if we are all very lucky, Uncle Giles will be home before us and cook the supper."

Smiling, Aunt Louise brought up the rear of the homeward procession. She was in a good mood, having had a peaceful afternoon in the restaurant while the children had amused themselves in the Theme Park. When at last they found their car, amongst what appeared to Sarah to be five thousand other cars, Aunt Louise asked her what she and Peter had enjoyed most about the place.

"The Cornish Museum, and looking at the rocks and cliffs by Lands End," Sarah answered.

"I liked the Pirate Ship play area," said Amy.

"I liked the gift shops," said Emma.

"And Peter, what did you like the best?" Aunt Louise asked again.

"Me, Oh, I liked the view of the lighthouse, and the ice cream parlour," he said.

Everyone laughed.

"Boys! Always thinking of their stomachs," said Aunt Louise, and they all laughed again.

Peter poked Sarah in the back. She looked at him with a frown that said:

"What's up?"

Peter gave her a long, large wink, that meant:

"I have a secret and will tell you about it later."

Then, as the car began to wend its way back home, Amy began to sing a curious version of an old song. It went like this:

"Row, row, row your boat, gently down the stream,
If you see a crocodile, remember just to scream!"

On the second time around, all four children joined in with the scream. The song continued and the screams became louder and louder, until Aunt Louise begged them to find something a little quieter to do.

Emma suggested: 'I spy with my little eye.' So they played that, until Peter said that he spied 'something beginning with H' and they saw that they were home.

Sarah fell out of the car yawning. Emma and Amy collected the picnic things from the car boot and took them indoors. Peter helped his Aunt with some of the things that were left in the car: deckchairs, Macs, rugs and toys. He gave Sarah some of the toys to carry. As they came to the end of the hallway, there stood Uncle Giles in the kitchen with a huge bowl of chips.

"Fish and Chips again, for which I make no apology. Fish, and sausages for Amy, are still in the oven. I had to keep them warm. I've been back from the *Fish and Chippery* for almost twenty minutes now. I thought you'd be back earlier."

"Oh, we've all had such a wonderful time, haven't we everyone!"

Aunt Louise looked round and smiled benevolently at her daughters and at Peter and Sarah.

"Now then, we had better eat straight away, before the fish and chips spoil. Just dump all the picnic stuff on the floor in the hall for now. Grab a knife and fork and let's everyone eat! Thank you so much, Giles dear, this is such a lovely surprise."

"No it isn't," Emma whispered behind her hand to Sarah, who was sitting next to her, "Dad often does this, to give Mum a cook's night off; he is really kind like that."

Silence followed this last remark, except for the occasional:

"Pass the salt and vinegar," or, "More Ketchup for me please," and, "Anyone for more of these lovely chips?"

To which the reply was invariably:

"Yes please!"

After supper, the girls helped their Mother clear the supper things away and Uncle Giles helped Peter put away the rugs, umbrellas and some of the toys. He asked if Sarah and he were having a good time.

"Oh, yes, thank you, we love it here. Sarah and I think that Cornwall is really great! I wish we could stay a bit longer," Peter said, and then went red with embarrassment.

He suddenly thought that, perhaps Aunt Louise and Uncle Giles might not want them for any longer.

"When do you leave us?" the Uncle enquired.

"On Saturday, by car, with Aunt Myf."

"Would you like to stay longer? I'm sure it could be arranged."

Peter went an even deeper crimson.

"No thanks. It's awfully kind of you, but Aunt Myf is expecting us for Easter Day and she would be terribly disappointed if we didn't go."

"Well then," smiled Uncle Giles, "perhaps another time. Pleased to have you, don't you know."

Uncle Giles smiled again, turned away and began to climb the stairs.

"Tell your Aunt that I'm about to run the bath for Amy."

"Yes Uncle, I will."

A much relieved Peter went off to find Aunt Louise. When he had delivered the message, then another one to tell Amy to be ready for her bath and bed time, Peter went to find Emma and Sarah. They were in the back garden, sitting on the bench that was under the palm tree. They were talking nineteen to the dozen.

"They look as thick as thieves. I am sure they are plotting something," Peter thought, and went immediately to join them.

"We've just been talking about the visit to the Stones," said Emma, looking up.

"And I know there's something else," added Sarah. "What was that *face* you made at me over the ice creams at Lands End, all about? Come on, big Bro. Spit it out and cough it up. We are dying to know."

"Well…"

"It's perfectly safe, Peter dear," said Emma, very seriously, "Daddy has got Amy in the bath and Mummy Dearest has gone to put her feet up and have a cup of tea. She'll be ever so tired after putting up with us all today."

"Come on, Peter, I know you've got something to say. Please don't keep us in *suspenders*, tell us right NOW!"

"OK, Emma, Sarah, it's like this; I felt something very strange happen when we were at the Stones."

"We thought you did. Is that why you asked us to go into the circle and you stayed outside?"

"Yes, I could see that you girls did not feel it at all, at least not in the same way that I did. I knew if there was anything in the centre of the Circle you would definitely find it. I also knew, or I suspected that if I went into the Stone Circle, I might just set something off that could be unpleasant. I decided it wasn't worth the risk. You did get a good look at everything, didn't you?"

"Oh yes," Emma said, "we took a really good look."

"But we didn't see any thing too strange," said Sara, "only the burnt patch that was in the middle and a bit off to one side. It was just like the newspaper said, when whatever it was caught fire."

"It all looked like someone had a bonfire there, that's all," Emma continued, "nothing particularly odd at all."

"Ah!" said Peter, "but wait till you hear what I found out at Lands End, while you lot were sorting out money for ice creams!"

Peter then went on to give the girls the description of the fiery monster with a beak, that he had overheard from Kevin.

"WOW!" said Sarah, when he had finished giving them the gory details, "this sounds serious."

"I don't know, sounds like a case of spontaneous combustion to me," Emma said in a very matter of fact way.

She was always most precise and liked to think that she approached problems in a scientific and analytical fashion.

"Can't have been," Peter returned, "because the man in the ice cream shop, Kevin, said that the THING came out of the Circle and then disappeared. No, I think Sarah is right. This IS serious and I think it is something that the Elves might be able to sort out."

"At least we can go and visit them next week when we get home," Sarah said cheerfully.

"Not until after Easter Day."

"Why is that Peter?" Emma asked.

"Because most of Sunday morning we'll be either getting ready for Church, going to Church..."

"And don't forget the Easter Eggs!"

"OK, Sarah, and Easter Eggs. But then it will be lunch time and after one of Aunt Myf's EXTRA special Sunday lunches, we'll all want to go to sleep and not go anywhere for the rest of the day. No, we shan't be able to get to the Elves until Monday at the very earliest."

Peter looked depressed.

"But at least Aunt Myf might drive you down to Arx Emain," Emma said comfortingly.

"There is that, Emma, but I have a very BAD feeling about all this. I had a bad feeling at the Stones. It was so awful, I can't begin to describe it to you. And I don't like the talk of this bird/horse THING. I don't know what it wants, or why it is here, but I think that it is evil. I also think that it has only started out on its business and I am quite sure that our policemen will not be able to stop it or deal with it in any way whatever."

"There's nothing you can do about it here and now," Sarah said, getting up from the bench, "and anyway, I don't see that it has anything to do with us."

Sarah made to go back indoors.

"I'm tired," she said, "I'm going to see if Amy has finished in the bath."

Sarah yawned loudly and left Emma and Peter to follow her later. They watched in silence as she went inside the house.

"I'm tired too," said Peter, resting his head in his hands.

"Hang on," said Emma, sounding excited, "can't you reach the Elves tele-pathetically?"

"*Telepathically.*"

"Telepathically, then. Can't you do that? I seem to remember that you said that you could send 'thought messages' to them, that summer Amy and I came to stay with you in Wales."

"We can, when we are at home, but Gwyn-ap-Nudd's Kingdom is not all that far away from our house. I really don't know if it would work from as far away as here."

"Well, Peter, can't you at least have a go at it? I'm sure it's not going to be safe round here with a monster like that on the rampage."

"Hmmm," said Peter, thoughtfully. "You might be right."

Something made him cast his mind back to the last time they had been on holiday in Greece. Gwyn-ap-Nudd, he remembered, had seemed to read his mind from as far away as Athens.

"Tell you what, we'll all get ready for bed and then have a meeting in your room. We could try sending a thought message all together. I can't guarantee it will work, though. It may just as quick to contact the Elves when we get home."

"But at least you'll have tried. Anyway, suppose this bird/horse THING does something awful before you get home?"

"Someone else will have to deal with it. I can't fight it, that's for sure! Come on Emma, let's go and see if the bathroom is free."

Peter got up from the bench and Emma followed him. Both going to find out if their ablutions could be made in order to get ready for bed. While Emma was cleaning her teeth, Peter told the others about the meeting and the proposed sending of a 'thought message'.

"How awfully exciting," said Amy, "when shall we do it?"

"Not too late, hopefully, or I shall be asleep."

Sarah cast herself down on her bed and shut her eyes.

"Come on, Sis, do keep awake. We'll need all the thought power we can get. If you do go to sleep, though, we'll have to carry on without you, that's all."

"But you can't do that."

"Oh yes we can."

That made Sarah sit up again. She rubbed her eyes and determined to keep herself awake, no matter what!

It was almost an hour later, when all four children were seated on the floor in Emma's room. Aunt Louise and Uncle Giles had bade them all: *a goodnight and pleasant dreams*, at least half an hour before. They were at this very moment relaxing in front of a most interesting programme on the television concerning tigers.

Amy wriggled on the floor. Half of her was off the rug and feeling most uncomfortable. The floor board beneath her squeaked.

"Ssh!" warned Emma.

"I'm not comfy."

"If you don't shut up," Peter told them, "your Mum and Dad will hear us and want to know what we're all doing here when we're supposed to be in bed."

Amy's lips began to quiver. Sarah frowned at Peter and gave her a hug.

"Look what you've done!" she said in a loud stage whisper, "now you've made Amy cry."

Amy buried her face in her comforter.

"Ssh!" said Peter.

"Ssh!" said Emma.

"Ssh, to you too!" retorted Sarah and if we're going to do this thought message thing, we had better be getting on with it."

"What do we do?" asked Amy, brightening up.

"We all sit here and think of Elves for at least five minutes," Peter told her, "that should do it."

"I'll time it on my watch," Sarah said, looking at the second hand. "Are we ready? GO!"

Everyone shut their eyes and thought ELVES and ARX EMAIN. Sarah's thoughts drifted. She opened her eyes for a second and checked her watch. Three minutes had gone. Only two more and she would at last be able to go to bed. She felt very, very tired. Sarah shut her eyes again. She could hear nothing except the others round her, breathing. Sarah tried hard to concentrate on her thoughts of Gwyn, Ederyn and the others.

One minute later, an unexpected scream rang out.

CHAPTER FOUR

Ederyn To The Rescue!

Peter, Emma and Amy leapt at once to their feet. Never mind Sarah who was laid out flat upon the floor of Emma's room. Fear of discovery made little geniuses of them all. Emma sent Amy to bed immediately and told her to look as if she were asleep.

"But don't snore, for goodness sake, or Mummy will find you out for sure."

Peter was shaking Sarah by the shoulders.

"Golly and gosh! I think she's out cold. She must have hit her head."

"Oh, my goodness! I hope it isn't concussion. Go in the bath room. Get my tooth mug and fill it with water. We'll try and get her round."

Peter flew off into the bathroom like lightning, his mind and stomach churning. Questions were bound to be asked. What were they to say in reply? He could already hear hurried footsteps coming up the stairs. As he came out of the bathroom with the mug of water, he met Aunt Louise on the landing.

"What on earth?"

"It's Sarah. I think she must have been sleepwalking."

Peter said this quite clearly and distinctly so that Emma might hear his excuse.

Aunt Louise ran into Emma's room.

"I just opened my eyes, and she was right here," said Emma, being moderately truthful.

"Sarah, Sarah!"

Aunt Louise called her name loudly in a frightened sort of way.

Fortunately, at that moment, Sarah opened her eyes.

"Ouch, my head, what happened?"

"You fainted," Peter explained.

"The dream, it came back! I saw the THING!"

"There, there," Aunt Louise stroked her forehead and then felt the rest of her head all over, "and by the feel of it you will have a nice big pigeon's egg, right here, by tomorrow morning," said Aunt Louise, finding a bump at the back. "Emma dear, you take your things into Amy's room and be with her tonight. Sarah had better stay here. I will have to keep a good eye on her."

Emma sloped off, muttering:

"Ugh," and, "Yuk!" at the thought of having to share a room with her little sister, but went to sleep in Amy's room all the same.

"Peter, do you have a torch?" asked Aunt Louise.

"Yes, I do."

"Well please go and fetch it, quickly now!"

Aunt Louise had once done a nursing course and was quite familiar with first aid procedures. When Peter returned with the torch, Aunt Louise shone it into Sarah's eyes, each in turn, to note any change in pupil reaction. All seemed well so far. Then she asked Sarah how she felt, to which the reply was:

"Fine, but scared."

"Very well. Sarah, I will stay with you for the present. Let's get you into bed. Peter, say goodnight to your sister."

Peter went over to Sarah, but as he kissed her on the forehead, she whispered:

"I saw the THING! It had a beak. It's that bird/horse beast from the stones, I know it is. I'm scared Peter. Do you think it's after us?"

"No, no," murmured her brother, "go to sleep Sis."

Peter then left her to the ministrations of their Aunt. Uncle Giles had also come to see what was going on. Peter heard them discussing whether to take Sarah to Casualty at the local Hospital, or not. He felt quite low and thoroughly dispirited. Instead of contacting the Elves, it somehow seemed as if the THING from the Stone Circle had managed to contact Sarah. Peter took himself off to bed. There was simply nothing else he could do!

In the morning, Peter awoke and went immediately to see Sarah. There she lay in Emma's bed, pale, but looking otherwise as bright as a button. Aunt Louise arrived with a tray of breakfast.

"If you manage to get this down," she said, "then we'll know that there's not much wrong with you."

She put the tray down on Sarah's knees, gave her a hug and left the room. Half a second later, Emma staggered in.

"Ugh!" she said, "fancy having to spend the night with one's sister, its worse than any monster, I can tell you!"

Then she looked at Sarah, who wore THAT look of fright again.

"Sorry, Sarah, That was a stupid thing to say. Don't go and faint on us again, will you. A lot of good that meeting did last night. It really was telepathetic, wasn't it! All we did was scare Sarah half to death, cause the grown-ups a load of agro, I've had to stay in Amy's room all night, and as yet," here she smiled a sarcastic smile at Peter, "I don't see any sign of any Elves. I'm off to breakfast!"

Emma stomped off down the stairs. She was evidently in a very bad mood. Amy appeared soon afterwards.

"Hello, everything alright? Good. I'm hungry and I smell toast. Are you coming down Peter?"

"In a minute."

"OK then, bye, bye."

Amy then zoomed off in her usual fashion. This morning she seemed astonishingly impervious to her sister's bad attitude.

"Well!" exclaimed Peter and threw up his hands.

"Can't you come and talk for a minute," Sarah asked, making space on the bed. "I'm quite alright now you know, honestly I am. I'm so sorry that I've been such a trouble."

"I knew that dream of yours meant something, I just knew it, and I did nothing about it. It's all my fault," Peter said squeezing her hand, "but it makes it all the more urgent that we get to see Anir, Gwyn, Ederyn or anyone from Arx Emain. I wish we were at home."

"In a way so do I, but I do like being here in Falmouth all the same. It looks as if it's going to be a lovely day. I wonder what we can do."

"Nothing much with you like this!"

"It was just a bit of a bump on the head."

"Yes, but you can see what Aunt Louise is like. She's a regular fussator. She has probably telephoned to Aunt Myf already to tell her all about it."

Sarah pouted and stabbed at her Cornflakes with the spoon.

"I'm going down to have my breakfast now. I'll find out what they want us to do today."

A tear began in the corner of Sarah's right eye. It was all going wrong. Their lovely holiday in Cornwall, which so far had been great fun, and now it looked as if she might have to waste a whole day of it in bed.

Over tea and eggs and bacon, it was decided to have a quiet day on the beach.

"We can do rock pools this morning, come home for lunch and go swimming, or paddling at least, in the afternoon. Can Sarah come with us, Mummy dear?" Emma asked eagerly.

"Not this morning."

Aunt Louise was quite firm.

"I'll see about it this afternoon. She watched Peter's face fall.

"Never mind, dear," she added kindly, "you still have Thursday and Friday with us. If Sarah keeps quiet today, I will look at the possibility of a boat trip for you all tomorrow."

"Hooray!" cried Amy, "Can I get down please? Let's go and get our beach things Emma. Come on Peter, we'll go and tell Sarah about the boat trip," and she was off like greased lightning upstairs to see the invalid, leaving Emma and Peter gasping.

It was no good. Aunt Louise could not be persuaded that Sarah should be anything but quiet that morning. Disconsolately, Peter bade her farewell half an hour later and followed Emma and Amy down to the rock pools. They caught a great many prawns, enough, almost, to cook up for tea; two baby crabs and a few small fish, but it was all no good. It just was not the same without Sarah.

Sarah meanwhile, was being very good. She returned to her own bed in Amy's room and went to sleep again. She half heard Uncle Giles leave for work and Aunt Louise using the vacuum cleaner in the sitting room. Then she noticed nothing more for at least an hour or so.

At eleven o'clock, Aunt Louise brought her up a drink of milk and some biscuits.

"You can be up for lunch, dear, if you feel like it. Then we shall see what we shall see."

The milk and biscuits disappeared. Aunt Louise returned to the kitchen to prepare the midday meal. Sarah heard the clatter of pots and pans and the sound of music on the radio. Then she heard an altogether different and unexpected noise: the sound of horse's hooves coming down the road in front of the house.

Something made Sarah leap out of bed to see what it was. Fortunately, Amy's room was in the front of the house. Sarah went straight to the window and looked out. She was almost shocked and very surprised to see who it was that was riding so calmly down the road towards her. For a moment, she forgot that probably only she might be able to see the rider and she looked up and down the road to see who else was watching. However, most people were already on the beach doing holiday things, as the day was already proving hotter than usual for spring.

Sarah wished with all her might that the others could be with her. She wondered how on earth her visitor could have arrived so quickly. She had also forgotten, momentarily, the awesome power of the Gardar Stone and its ability to provide the Elves and their friends the convenience of instantaneous travel, time travel and other benefits. As soon as the rider appeared outside the front gate, Sarah called to him as loudly as she could without attracting attention.

"Ederyn, Ederyn, Oh I'm so glad it's you!"

Ederyn waved to her, dismounted and tying his horse to the garden fence, leapt effortlessly over the gate and ran up the path to stand directly under the bedroom window. Sarah leaned out as far as she dare.

"Oh Ederyn, you can't imagine how glad I am to see you. But how did you come here so quickly?"

"Through the power of the Gardar Stone, of course, but you should know that by now, dear Sarah."

Ederyn bowed low to her. Sarah was once again impressed by the extreme delicacy of manners that belonged to the Elf people.

"We received your call for help. Though Gwyn-ap-Nudd has known of the trouble down here for some time. We did not know that you had become involved with it, however."

"We are and we aren't," Sarah told him, "I can't really explain everything from up here, and I can't come down because I've had an accident. I bumped my head and Aunt says I must stay in bed this morning."

"I am very sorry to hear that."

"Have you seen the others?"

"You mean Peter and those cousins of yours?"

"Yes, they ought to be somewhere on the beach. They are trawling the rock pools until lunchtime."

"I will go immediately and see if I can find them. Thank you Sarah."

And before Sarah could say anything else, Ederyn had leapt over the gate again and on to his horse. She watched as he trotted round towards the cliff walk where there were bushes and small trees enough to hide a horse. Anxiously, she went back to bed to wait for the others to return and, hopefully make their report.

Half past eleven, quarter to twelve, ten to twelve, the minutes dragged by. Then Sarah heard footsteps outside and, Oh joy, horse's hooves with them! Below, there were suddenly animated voices.

"Good," she thought, "Ederyn has found them at least. Now we'll see what's what."

The front door opened, the feet tramped inside loudly and the sound of horse's hooves trotted away.

Sarah couldn't wait to know what had been happening, But just as she had decided to go to the top of the stairs, Aunt Louise appeared with a tray of lunch. Sarah was deeply disappointed.

"There we are dear. Perhaps you would like to get up this afternoon, after you have eaten your lunch and had a little nap. I am going to feed the others now. They must have had a very good morning, they are so lively now they've come back."

Aunt Louise then left Sarah to toy with a piece of plaice and mashed potato. As soon as lunch was decently over, Peter raced up the stairs, followed closely by Emma and Amy.

"Don't worry, Mummy, we'll get Sarah's tray for you," Amy shouted back, as her mother was about to protest that what Sarah needed was peace, and quiet, and rest.

When they all arrived in the bed room, to their surprise, Sarah was already up and dressed.

"I am quite alright now, truly I am!" she said.

"First things first," Emma said, "Amy, take that tray down for Mummy."

"But Emma..."

"Just go!"

Amy went.

"What happened?" Sarah could wait no longer.

"Ederyn came to look for us on the beach. He said he had seen you too," began Peter.

"But we couldn't speak properly, not with me leaning out of a window."

"I told him everything, about your dream and all about the monster that frightened the Sympathetic Earthers and fried their dogs."

"Poor Rex!" said Emma, in such a sad voice that it made everyone laugh.

Amy reappeared in the doorway. Peter continued:

"Ederyn says that he will stay around here until we go home, as our guard, just in case."

"Just in case, in case of what?" Sarah asked, sounding rather worried.

"In case the THING decides to pay Falmouth a visit, but I gather that Ederyn thinks it unlikely."

Sarah went pale, Emma shivered and Amy's lower lip wobbled.

"Look, Amy's about to cry. Come here, little darling," Sarah stretched out her arms, "sit with me and don't worry."

"I don't want the nasty big monster to find me," sniffed Amy, desperately searching for her comforter.

"It won't, I promise," said Peter, "Ederyn is here now. Everything is going to be alright."

Amy stopped sniffing and Peter went on with his report.

"Ederyn says that Anir will meet us as soon as we get home, probably on the beach at Newport. I said I would go there on the way to Aunt Myf's. Otherwise, he will come to us."

"Do you think Aunt Myf will want to stop on the way home after such a long journey?" said Sarah.

"Maybe not, but she might if we tell her why. You know what a *good egg* she is. Ederyn said that Gwyn suspects that the Elves have met this particular monster before, a long, long time ago. It came differently then. Gwyn thinks that the THING last appeared as a great Boar. It caused all kinds of trouble and killed quite a few of Emperor Arthur's warriors, including one of his sons. Gwyn was involved in getting rid of it and personally, with Arthur and others, chased it into the sea, somewhere quite near here, actually. It had never been seen since, not until now that is."

"Does this THING have a name?" asked Emma.

"It certainly does. If it is what Gwyn and Ederyn think it is. Then it is called in Welsh: the Twrch Trwyth, or more usually the Troynt. It is known to be a destructive monster of the worst kind. It can decimate whole towns at once!"

"Gosh," said Sarah, "we knew it was bad, frying those poor little doggies like that. Hmmm, the Troynt in the Circle."

"Yes, I rather gathered from Ederyn that it is like a mini war machine all on its own," said Peter with a grim smile.

"Don't you think we should warn the authorities?" asked Emma.

"I think they already know," Peter waved the morning newspaper at her. "Look! Just read the headlines on the front page."

"ARSON ATTACKS ON LOCAL FARMS," Emma read.

"Wow," said Amy, "Do you think that's the work of the beast?"

"I'm almost sure it is," Peter replied, "see, down at the bottom of page two, there is a description of sheep being all burnt up in a field, two of the farmers also said that they noticed a dark cloud coming towards them before the fires broke out. Some claim that it was some sort of freak weather condition, caused by the unusual heat during this last week, but WE know better! Hey, Amy, why have you got your fingers in your ears?"

"I don't want to hear about the monster."

"Never mind, Amy," said Sarah, "it seems to be going away from here. If you had read on a bit, Peter, you would have noticed that the last farm in the report lies well to the north of here, near Perranporth, almost Newquay in fact."

Amy removed her fingers from her ears and cheered up immediately.

"Hooray, hooray, it's going away," she sang.

Peter frowned.

"*If* we see Ederyn again, we must tell him about this; though he did say, most positively, that if he does not see us before we get home, we *must* find Anir and report to him. He will probably be waiting for us on Newport beach."

"If we see Ederyn," repeated Sarah, "but he'll probably get to know anyway, Elves always do, by one means or another. But now, you lot, I'm feeling perfectly fine. I'm going to ask if I can come down to the beach with you. It's such a lovely day that it would be a shame if I missed it. I fancy having an ice cream, a great big one, three scoops at least."

Sarah got up from the bed and looked round at the others.

"Come on then," she said, "you've had your rest, let's all go now," and off she went to persuade Aunt Louise of her very great need of fresh, sea air.

They finally got on to the beach at half past two and spent the rest of the afternoon there. Peter, Emma and Amy tried the water and although it was rather on the cold side, they did get in and go swimming. After the general consumption of spectacular ice creams, Sarah amused herself by looking for shells and other treasure, as she sat in the shade of some rocks.

No more did they see of Ederyn that day, nor the next. The newspapers continued to print lurid headlines. A caravan site had come under fire, literally! The terrified residents described a whirlwind or tornado that roared through their camp. It must have been an electrical storm too, they all said, for several caravans had been set alight and some men had been beaten up by the whirlwind, so they said. These ghastly occurrences had taken place just north of Bodmin.

"Well, at least it's still going away from here," said Sarah thankfully.

"Yes, but WHERE is it going?" asked Peter. "It looks now as if it is on its way somewhere, but where and why?"

For this question, no-one save the beast could have any answer.

This next day, Aunt Louise had insisted that Sarah be kept quiet again, but she promised that on the final day of Peter and Sarah's visit they would have a boat trip to St. Maws. Thursday, then was spent upon the beach once more, to which nobody had any objection. This time, however, Sarah was allowed to swim with the others, a bracing experience! They were watched over by Aunt Louise, who brought knitting, a magasine and a picnic tea with her.

Friday, the last day in Cornwall for Peter and Sarah, all four children were taken to the ferry pier in Falmouth. Then, at last they set sail for St. Maws. A fish and chip lunch, everyone's favourite, (except for Amy!) was had in the pretty little town. Then they all went to search for souvenirs and postcards.

"I always like to have some cards to send and some to keep, to remind me of where I have been," said Sarah.

"Why can't you remember where you've been anyway?" said Peter cheekily, "boy, oh boy! Have you got a poor memory!"

He darted away as Sarah made as if to slap him on the back with her postcards.

On their return to Falmouth, there was still no sign at all of Ederyn, so they assumed that there could be no imminent danger.

"Perhaps he is tailing that *Twerp Trick*," said Amy, managing to mispronounce the monster's name.

"You make Ederyn sound like a Detective," said Peter, "but I guess he might be doing something like that."

They were in Amy's room, helping Sarah to pack. It was an occasion that gathered in gloom and solemnity as time went by and the case was filled. By bed time, all the four of them were quite subdued and low in spirits.

"I don't want you to go," Amy said and jumped on Sarah, hugging her tight.

Then she hugged Peter. Even Emma gave her a hug.

"Time for bed," Aunt Louise called from the doorway, "you have a long journey ahead of you tomorrow, Peter, Sarah, then all the joys of Easter. Aunt Myf will be here as soon as she can in the morning, so you must be ready to go with her straight away."

She wished them all goodnight and left the children to their slumbers, which this night remained undisturbed. Then she returned to her kitchen where she prepared food for the travellers.

"It is a very long way back for them, all that way to Pembrokeshire," she said to herself, as she began to slice a loaf up for sandwiches.

The following morning, Aunt Myf arrived earlier than expected. Sarah and Peter were ready for her, even so. They were disappointed in their last minute plans as they had hoped for a last look at the beach, and perhaps a last look for Ederyn. But there it was; half past ten saw them seated in Aunt Myf's car, surrounded by luggage, the inevitable picnic lunch and their toys and souvenirs.

"Goodbye!" called Aunt Louise and Uncle Giles.

"Goodbye!" yelled Emma and Amy.

"And don't forget to let us know all about, *you know what*," Emma hissed at them through the front passenger window.

"We won't," Sarah and Peter replied. Aunt Myf started the car and they were on their way.

"Straight up the Motorway, over the Severn Bridge and across the Brecon Beacons, I think," said Aunt Myf, "then we shall get home in time for supper, I hope."

She continued, with an air of great confidence.

Peter and Sarah looked at each other. Through the make-up mirror on the passenger sun flap, Sarah raised her eyebrows at Peter. Was he going to tell Aunt Myf about the beastly Troynt, Twrch Trwyth, whatever it called itself, or not? And if so, how much of Ederyn's information and his own wild guesses was he about to impart?

CHAPTER FIVE

A Meeting With Anir

Aunt Myf put the car radio on, as she usually did on a long journey. A merry air by Delibes played them through Truro. Sarah was on tenterhooks. She kept looking at Peter. Was he or wasn't he going to tell Aunt Myf what had been going on this past week? It was not until Aunt Myf had turned on to the Motorway that Peter began to speak.

"Aunt Myf,"

"Yes dear."

"I have a surprise for you."

"That's nice, dear, but I have one for you."

Aunt Myf drove steadily on down the Motorway.

"I know exactly what has been going on in Cornwall and that you seem to have some kind of involvement with it!"

Peter and Sarah listened, quite stunned by her knowledge.

"What is it about you two?" she asked, "you seem to attract trouble! We can't leave you on your own for two minutes without something happening that requires the full attention of all those at Arx Emain."

Peter was so taken aback by these words that he just sat next to his Aunt, opening and shutting his mouth like a goldfish.

Sarah cut in:

"How do you know about it?" she asked.

"I have my methods," Aunt Myf replied mysteriously.

Then she smiled.

"Actually, Anir came and told me all about everything. Just appeared suddenly, like he usually does, out of the blue. I was in the garden hanging out some washing, when I heard footsteps coming down the path by the side of the house. That's funny, I said to myself, it's not time for Tomos to come home from work. And while I'm wondering about it, and pegging up a towel, up pops Anir, as large as life and twice as natural, as they say."

"But what did he say?"

"I was coming to that, Peter dear.

"Hello," he said.

Then I said *hello* and I asked him about his family.

"They are well," he replied to me.

Then I said:

"Haven't seen you around for a while."

Then he said:

"I have been busy. Gwyn has been to his Kindred over the seas and I have had to keep watch alone."

"Where's Ederyn then," I asked."

Aunt Myf patted the side of her nose with her right forefinger.

"I'm canny like that you see," she said, "I know that when Gwyn is away, it is usually Anir AND Ederyn who are left in charge, though Anir has been in charge alone quite a few times."

"So?" asked Sarah, "what did he say to that?"

"Ederyn has gone South," he told me, "there is trouble in Cornwall. A few Elves still dwell there, but in the depths of the countryside as they are few, and not so well organised as we are in Arx Emain."

"So you're an Elf now?"

I teased him and he blushed. He didn't say anything, but went on to say:

"There is a beast loose in Cornwall and it is on its way North."

Of course I asked him what it was.

"The Twrch Trwyth," he said.

Now even I have heard of that! You see, all my meetings with the Celtic History Society have had some use after all. I am sure I have read about it in a book once too."

"Look, Aunt Myf," Peter suddenly pointed at a Motorway sign, "South Wales and the Severn Bridge coming up."

"Oh yes, thank you dear." Aunt Myf turned the wheel and put the car in the correct lane for Wales.

"Not long now and we'll be over the border and in Chepstow. I think we shall visit the Hotel there and have an early lunch."

"But what did Anir say about the monster?"

"Oh, sorry Sarah, I was telling you about Anir, wasn't I. Well, he just said that it need not concern me for the moment but that you two were quite near to where it started off. Then he told me to watch the news in the newspapers.

"I am keeping an extra eye out for trouble here," he said. "Ederyn has gone to see where it goes next. Keep your eyes open, Myfanwy, and hope that it is not coming here."

"I will keep a good look out," I said.

Then I invited him in for a cup of tea and some Bara Brith, and we talked about something else entirely."

"I wonder where he has got to now?" said Peter, gazing out of the car window. The bright farmlands of the Severn estuary were passing by them in a flash.

"Look!" Sarah shouted out suddenly.

"Where, what?" said Peter.

"Don't frighten the driver, I might crash if you shout at me like that again," said Aunt Myf fiercely.

"Sorry, Aunty. But I say, just look down there Peter."

To their left, beneath one of the Motorway bridges that passed over a small stream, were the remains of a burnt out farmstead. Sarah and Peter looked at each other in horror. It could not be, could it?

"That beastly Troynt must be able to move pretty fast if it can get as far as here in such a short space of time," whispered Peter.

"What are you looking at?" Aunt Myf asked.

"The farm down there, it looked all burnt up."

"Are you sure?"

"Quite!"

"Tell you what," said Peter, "why don't we buy a newspaper in Chepstow and see what it says."

"Very well, Peter dear, we shall do just that."

Aunt Myf drove the car at flying speed past the last Motorway sign for South Wales and the Severn Bridge.

"At last," thought Sarah, "nearly across the borders, then we're home!"

Soon enough they were crossing the bridge. Spirits rose at the thought of luncheon and it was not long afterwards that Aunt

Myf was parking her car in the car park of the big Hotel in Chepstow.

Aunt Myf led Peter and Sarah into the dining room, where they ordered and ate a lunch that was definitely more than a snack.

"And we've still got Aunt Louise's sandwiches to eat yet," said Sarah, finishing off a chocolate ice cream.

"We'll keep those for tea," said Aunt Myf happily. "Now Peter, I see you have finished your pudding. What about your kind offer to go and buy us a newspaper? Thank you so much, dear," she said as Peter rose from his seat at the table and left for the shop.

Fifteen minutes later, Peter, Sarah and Aunt Myf were in the lounge of the big Hotel with the paper spread out all over the floor as they tried to find what they were looking for.

"There's nothing in my bit," said Sarah.

"Nor mine," said Aunt Myf.

"Nor mine either," said Peter.

In fact, there were no mentions at all of anything odd or untoward.

"That farm must have got burnt up some time ago," Sarah remarked.

"But it did look like recent damage," Peter said.

"We'll just have to keep our eyes well open, that's all," said Aunt Myf, "are you all ready? Then it's over the Brecon Beacons and home. Come on!"

The three travellers found the next stage of their journey quite uneventful. There were no burnt out farms in the Brecon Beacons, not so much as a singed hedgerow or forest fire. Tea time, with the sandwiches provided by Aunt Louise was had at Lampeter. So the journey passed on, until they had crossed the Afon Teifi and were back on home ground, driving along roads that were familiar to them. Aunt Myf drove through Nevern and straight on to Newport. She had already parked the car on the drive, when Sarah remembered something.

"Bother!"

"What? Oh goodness, I've forgotten too," said Peter.

"What are you two on about now?"

"We've forgotten Anir," wailed Sarah, "we told Ederyn that we'd meet him on the beach!"

"Well, I'm not going now."

"Please, Aunty Dearest..."

"No Peter, and no amount of flattery will make me go. Look, here's my Tomos with Catrin now. Get your bags and baggages and take them into the house. Step lively now!"

Dolefully, Sarah and Peter took their gear inside, while Aunt Myf received an enthusiastic greeting from Catrin and a relieved one from Uncle Tomos, who said:

"She's been a little pickle, dear, a little pickle all day!"

Sarah and Peter took their cases upstairs. In Aunt Myf's house they had to share a room. Neither viewed sharing with Catrin something to be contemplated. She was too young, as yet.

"When she is a little older, I will share," Sarah told Aunt Myf, and they left it at that.

"What are we going to do?" Peter was saying, when Aunt Myf opened the bedroom door.

"Ssh, listen..." she looked round at the children, "Anir is not stupid. He may wait on the beach a bit today but not for too long, I expect. He knows that you are coming here, so I expect he will catch up with you both tomorrow. That is if the situation is so urgent that he needs to see you immediately. After all, nothing much seems to be going on around here, does it?"

"No, Aunt Myf."

"So then, come on down and have your supper. Tomos has made a huge pile of spaghetti, the dear man, you'll love it!"

And so passed Saturday evening. Everything was quiet. Sunday was Easter day and all business had stopped for the holiday celebrations. Peter was right in supposing that most of the morning would be taken up with the Church service, though the Hymns were most uplifting and some quite jolly! Everyone departed afterwards for lunch in very good spirits.

"And now for the Easter Eggs!" cried Uncle Tomos gleefully, as he drove everyone home.

"Boy beg?" asked Catrin.

"No, no, darling," said Aunt Myf, "not *boiled* egg, Easter eggs, great big CHOCOLATE ones. We'll have them after our lunch."

Luncheon was cooking slowly in the oven, so that by some miracle, (the usual one that occurred most Sundays in Aunt Myf's house) when they arrived back from Church, most of lunch was ready to serve out.

"I'm full," said Sarah, when she had done as much justice to the turkey and trifle as anyone could.

"So am I," said Peter. "I couldn't eat another thing."

But then of course he did, because out came the Easter Eggs and Peter certainly managed to do justice to *them!*

As Aunt Myf began to take the dirty dishes through to the kitchen, she said:

"Why don't you two take Catrin for a walk in her pram. She needs her fresh air and I am sure you could do with a walk to shake things down, after all you've eaten today!"

Peter and Sarah were not pleased. Walking Catrin round Newport was not their idea of fun on an Easter Sunday afternoon. Miserably they went obediently to get the pram. Aunt Myf went to get Catrin ready. She had to be taken into the bathroom, for a deal of chocolate egg seemed to cover most of her!

When Aunt Myf brought her daughter down again, she found a glum looking pair. Peter and Sarah were waiting in the hall with the pram, which was one of the old fashioned bassinet variety, and Catrin's favourite turquoise rug.

"Why so depressed?" their Aunt enquired, "get along with you. You don't know WHO you might meet on a walk, do you?"

Aunt Myf tucked Catrin into her pram and wished Peter and Sarah goodbye.

They were down the front path and out of the gate before they knew what they were doing. Suddenly Peter brightened up.

"We're slow today," he said.

"Why?"

"Aunt Myf was telling us that we shall very probably meet Anir if we go out for a walk."

A smile spread over his sister's face as the penny dropped.

"Look Sarah... Anir couldn't pop up when Uncle Tomos is at home, not looking as he usually does. He'd probably get arrested for loitering with intent."

"Yes, he does usually look pretty scruffy."

"So Aunt Myf thinks that he's possibly in town..."

"Or on the beach! Come on Peter, what are we waiting for? Let's go and look, I bet he's there!"

And Sarah sped away with Catrin looking quite astonished as the pram went faster and faster past the shops and down to the sea. Peter followed them as quickly as he could, but the pram pulled Sarah on, quicker and quicker.

"Careful!" he shouted, "You'll upset Catrin."

But Sarah did not upset the pram or Catrin. Somehow, she, the pram and its precious contents arrived safe and sound on Newport sands. Sarah leant on the side of the pram, panting and trying to catch her breath. Peter ran on to the sands to join her.

"I say, you were in a bit of a hurry, what on earth possessed you? That was a completely idiotic thing to do with a baby. You really ought to be more careful with Catrin, she might have been badly injured if she had fallen out."

He turned to address the infant.

"Hi, little one, I hope you're alright!"

"More chocky!" was all he got in reply.

"Have you got any, Sarah?"

"No, oh, I don't know though. Hang on a min. I might have some in my coat pocket."

Peter picked up a piece of seaweed and waved it over his head to amuse Catrin, while Sarah searched for the chocolate. When it was found and Catrin was happy, Peter and Sarah looked all around them, to see if Anir might be any where on the sands.

The sun shone brightly through fluffy spring clouds. Blue sky was reflected in the various pools that spread across the beach. The tide was out, leaving the sands to their low tide inhabitants. A small crab scuttled past Peter's left foot.

"I can't see Anir anywhere," he said. "There's only us and a few more on the beach today, tourists maybe. You must be wrong, Sarah, I don't think Anir can be coming here after all."

"I am, I have and I'm here!" said a voice behind them.

Thankfully, Sarah turned round to see, by now, the familiar sight of Anir in his woefully battered old cloak, looking more like a tramp than ever, she thought. No, it would not have done to introduce Anir to Uncle Tomos looking like this, his Detective's mind would have him all boxed up in the 'usual suspects' or 'suspicious individuals' department. Perhaps if Anir were smarter...

"Hello Anir," said Peter, breaking into Sarah's reverie.

"So!" said Anir, "you have given up your festive celebrations this afternoon just to come and see me, Eh?"

"Well, not exactly, though I suppose, yes maybe," said Sarah, blushing.

"We have things to tell you, important things that I think the Lord Gwyn must know about at once!" Peter said.

"About this?"

They saw that Anir had a copy of The Welsh Daily News in his hand.

"Have a look at this, here on the front page."

Sarah took the newspaper with trembling hands:

"Look at this, Peter, look, it's coming closer!"

"Oh my, oh my!" exclaimed Peter, as he quickly scanned the headlines. They proclaimed in bright red ink:

"ARSONIST STRIKES AGAIN!"

Beneath was the story, describing how a mad arsonist was *blazing a trail...*

"Almost funny, that," said Sarah, "I wonder who writes this stuff?"

...from the Severn estuary, past the Brecon Beacons and all through central Wales! It attacked a pig-sty here, a hay barn there. The last town to be mentioned was Llandeilo on the River Tywi.

"It certainly seems to be coming our way," said Anir, peering over Peter's shoulder. "Or it may turn and go south again, or north, who can say? If you want to give Gwyn all your information and hear more on the subject, you had best come to the meeting tomorrow. Gwyn has called all the Watchers to appear before the full council."

"It has been extraordinarily active and seems to move at amazing speeds. There was nothing in the news yesterday, we checked," Peter went on.

"It is gaining strength," Anir told him, "it is known to be a destroyer of property and land, but it also has a voracious appetite and will eat ANYTHING in its path!"

Sarah gulped:

"Anything?" she asked.

"ANYTHING!" Anir repeated. "If it should come as far as here, and I have had intimations from The Lord Gwyn that it is more than likely that it may; we must be ready for it. Unchecked, it could devastate a whole area. That is why Gwyn has called an extraordinary council meeting for tomorrow. As our special friends you might have been invited anyway, but as you have information to give on the subject, and we already knew that from Ederyn, I think it is vital that you attend."

"I don't know if you will think much of what I learned," Peter said, "I got it all from someone in the Sympathetic Earth Movement."

"Ederyn is of the opinion that your information *is* useful and Gwyn himself must hear what you have to say. You all visited the site where the Troynt came to life, so to speak, did you not?"

"Yes, but..." began Peter.

"There wasn't much to see, honest," Sarah said.

"Ah yes," Anir replied, "but there are also feelings and impressions that must be gone into. We shall see then what we shall see," he said mysteriously. "Also, there is something *you* must hear, Peter, that might turn out to your advantage. Anyway, the Lord Gwyn has returned but lately from a visit over the seas and he needs to have all the facts on the beast. Will you come to the meeting?"

Anir said this last quite forcefully, almost as if it were a command. Something told Peter he had better sit up and pay attention. He began to think of The Tests again.

"We will, if Aunt Myf is willing and able to bring us to you," Peter told him.

"She is. I spoke to her earlier," said Anir, "she is willing to be involved, for the present at least, but she does not want to be mixed up in the Elves' business quite as much as you two do!" Anir smiled broadly. "Good! So, that's settled then. I shall see you next at Arx Emain."

"When is the meeting?" Peter asked.

"Good point. At noon Peter, for it is not good to talk of matters of evil, such as this Troynt, when the light of the sun has faded and the dark is upon us."

"We'll be there, I promise," said Peter.

He suddenly felt a thrill pass through his body at the thought of actually going to the Council of the Elves.

"And who knows to what that might lead," he thought, as he remembered once more, that certain little thing about the special trials which he knew led to *The Guardianship*.

"Onta more chocky!" said a sleepy little voice.

Catrin, who had been asleep, had now woken up and wanted food and attention.

"Oh my goodness!" Sarah looked at her watch, "it's four o'clock, your tea time already little one. We'd better go Anir, bye."

Sarah began to manoeuvre the large pram off the beach and back to the paved streets of Newport town. Peter helped her, for pushing and pulling a bassinet pram with a heavy toddler inside can be a tricky business.

When they were on terra firma once more, Peter looked back to wave goodbye to their friend, but Anir had gone.

"Disappeared again," he said, "let's get on Sarah and get home. I'm not hungry yet but I could do with a drink."

"Me too," Sarah murmured, "me too!"

They continued then, to make a good effort at pushing the bassinet as fast as possible back to Aunt Myf's house, where they found that Uncle Tomos was still 'resting his eyes' (his euphemism for a good nap!) in the study and Aunt Myf was putting finishing touches to her Easter Cake.

After tea, Peter and Sarah went up to the guest bedroom to talk.

"I expect that Aunt Myf has already made her own arrangements for tomorrow," Peter began.

"I expect so."

"That THING is moving jolly fast, much, much quicker than I ever imagined."

"Yes, it is isn't it."

"To think that it was in Cornwall when we were, and now it's on it's way here."

"Don't remind me," said Sarah, making a *face,* "But how do they know that it's coming here? How do you?"

"Well, I'm sure of it, I just FEEL it! I bet Gwyn and the others do too, that's why he is calling the extraordinary meeting of the Council."

"Well, I don't feel anything, except perhaps angry that yet another monster is having to be got rid of. Why, oh why, do they all want to come here?"

"That is a very interesting question, Sis. Why DO they all want to come here? Why are the Elves here? Why are all those Ancient Monuments here? Especially: why is everything that is magic centred round here?"

"It can't be only here," Sarah argued, "because the Lord Gwyn goes over the seas; to Ireland I presume, to his kindred there. We also know that he goes to the north, to the Mountains of Snowdonia I think."

"Well, both of those places are certainly stuffed full with magic," Peter said again.

"True, so why don't the monsters go there for a change?"

"Perhaps some of them do, only we don't hear about it. Perhaps we only know about the ones that we are involved with, I don't know!"

Sarah had a thought:

"You don't suppose it has anything to do with that prison, or kingdom of Arddu? You know the monster who was buried under the Prescelly Mountains; the one that was killed by Anir and the Samildanach. Mightn't there be some of his creatures left under there? If there are, they might get strong and powerful again. The whole place is obviously a great centre for magic. Perhaps they are coming out of there or are attracted by the place."

"Maybe," Peter said, "I used to think I was an expert on Elves and their doings, but now I'm not so sure. I think there is an awful lot to learn about them and the world that they live in. One day..."

Peter paused as he looked at the time on his travel clock. He did not finish what he was going to say. He did not want to give away just yet, how eager he was to join their world!

"Come on Sarah," he said then, "let's go and have a game of cards with Uncle Tomos. I think it's time he was woken up."

The rest of Easter Day was spent quietly. The next morning was of course, a Bank Holiday, but Uncle Tomos said that he had an urgent case to attend to at the Police station, something that would not wait, so he went into work as usual.

"I'll go in, I have to, Dearest," he said to Aunt Myf, "but I shall try to get away early if at all possible."

They kissed each other goodbye, and Uncle Tomos went out and off to work.

Aunt Myf sighed.

"I *shall* look forward to the day he retires!" she said emphatically, and went to fetch Catrin, who was making a big mess out of a boiled egg.

Sarah and Peter could hear their Aunt 'tut-tutting' in the kitchen, as they skulked around in the hall, waiting to find out what was going to happen next.

Suddenly, Aunt Myf shot out of the kitchen and up the stairs with Catrin under one arm.

"What a mess!" she said, "Bathroom for you, my little poppit."

Then she turned round at the top of the stairs and called to her niece and nephew:

"Peter, Sarah, if you want to go to this Elves' meeting, you had better get ready too, and be quick about it!"

Peter and Sarah looked at each other. Then, without saying anything, shrugged their shoulders, raised their eyes heavenwards and followed their Aunt upstairs.

Half an hour later, all four were washed and dressed and ready for anything. Aunt Myf put Catrin, Sarah and Peter in her car and went to check if she had left the gas on, the TV on, or a window open. Then she solemnly locked the front door. It was while she was engaged upon her duties that a shadowy figure came up the garden path. It was Anir. He was carrying the mail AND the daily papers!

"I thought you would like to see these before you go," he said.

"Dear me, cousin Anir, you gave me quite a fright there, nearly a heart attack, creeping up on me like that! What is it now?"

"Special Edition! The Troynt seems to have reached Carmarthen. There have been several places attacked all around the river Tywi, each attack gaining in ferocity."

Anir gave the papers to Aunt Myf, who glanced at them briefly.

"So, we had best get on," she said. "Are you wanting a lift down with us?"

Anir thanked her and said that he would be grateful. As she drove out from her house, Aunt Myf passed the papers to Peter and Sarah. They looked at the headlines but made no comment. It was all too awful! Then they both remained silent for the duration of the journey to Arx Emain. This was not difficult, for Aunt Myf made continuous conversation with Anir about everything and anything; the weather and family matters figuring large amongst her subject matter!

They passed Wolf's Castle, a familiar landmark on the road between Fishguard and Haverfordwest. It was also the sign that they were nearing the outskirts of the underground Kingdom of Gwyn-ap-Nudd, Arx Emain itself.

Peter found that he was feeling quite excited. The Easter holidays were indeed looking up. The opportunity for REAL adventure, and perhaps another of those *Tests,* was now a definite possibility! Another little shiver of electricity wriggled down his spine and he smiled at the thought of seeing Lord Gwyn and the Elves again. Sarah, on the other hand was not feeling quite as enthusiastic.

"How weird some grown-ups are," she mused, "and Aunt Myf and Anir are definitely two of the very weirdest that I have ever met. They never do what one expects they ought to do. Here is Aunt Myf driving us all to a meeting with The Elves, when by rights she, and even we, ought not to be getting involved with them or the monsters. I bet that she wants to see what is going on as much as Peter does. The only thing is, I'm not awfully sure I do. I do hope there won't be too much fighting THIS time."

Aunt Myf parked her car near a bus stop. She felt that it was safe if it could be seen from the road. Everyone got out. Catrin began to complain immediately, so aunt Myf gave her a biscuit.

"Wholemeal, very healthy, she really loves them," Aunt Myf explained to Anir, who had wondered aloud if his little son, Dylan, would like such a thing.

Aunt Myf provided Anir with one or two on the spot, wrapped up in foil.

"Let Dylan try them and see," she said, "I am sure he will like them."

Anir led everyone into the scrub land that lay beyond the road. They had not gone far, when he gave three whistles. Horses ready tacked-up appeared as if from nowhere, one each.

"You are old enough to ride alone now," said Anir, "and we have horses a plenty at Arx Emain. Let us go swiftly now, for time is running on. Mount up Peter, Sarah and Myfanwy. Shall I take Catrin, or shall you manage?"

"She will go in the baby carrier on my back, thank you kindly, Anir," said Aunt Myf.

"Then we shall be off and away. The Meeting will start directly at noon and we must not be over late. Come 'hup' you horses and trot on!"

Anir led them away at as brisk a pace as could be managed in the circumstances. So the party made their way to the doors of Arx Emain that are hidden to all save those who know.

As they arrived, the Great Door swung open and the horses passed straight into the paved outer hall. They were greeted at once by several Elves who took the horses away and hurried their visitors down the main tunnel to the Great Hall where the Lord Gwyn-ap-Nudd awaited their presence in order that the reports concerning the Troynt should be complete.

It had been quite a while since Peter, Sarah and Aunt Myf had been in the Elf Kingdom. They were once more impressed by the sheer beauty of the place. The wonderful carvings in stone that made forests and fields, sea and sky come to life in the home of the Elves. Not to mention all the birds and beasts that were also hewn to such perfection on walls and ceilings and doors, that when one looked closely, you might almost expect to see them move! Sarah explained it once to Emma rather like this:

"I suppose if the Elves don't go out of their Kingdom very much, then at least they have most of the outside things inside with them, even if they are carvings made of stone."

Aunt Myf, Catrin and Anir had arrived at the entrance to the Great Hall. They stopped there, for Gwyn-ap-Nudd was speaking to the assembled Elves. Peter and Sarah peered round them, trying to see what was going on. Then they heard themselves being addressed.

"Come in Peter, Sarah, Myfanwy. Our greeting to you, friends of Arx Emain, and welcome to our Council Meeting!" said the Lord Gwyn.

CHAPTER SIX

The Watchers Report

Anir led the visitors directly to the dais, where sat the King of the Elves with the chiefest of his court. They were not surprised to see that Aneryn was there with her son, Dylan. Aunt Myf curtseyed to Lord Gwyn and then removed the baby carrier with Catrin in it.

"You are getting much too big to go in this," she muttered under her breath.

Then she patted Catrin forwards towards the Elf child, who was playing at Aneryn's feet with some brightly coloured shapes. They looked interesting to Catrin and she ran eagerly to join him in his play.

Peter and Sarah noticed four empty seats to the right of where Aneryn sat, and the Lord Gwyn directed his visitors to be seated therein. They took their seats forthwith and the meeting of the Elves was properly begun.

"Welcome again to our visitors, who have come to join us here at Arx Emain for this Extraordinary Council. Now that we are all gathered, we shall proceed with the usual reports, beginning with those who patrol the lands closest to Arx Emain."

A short, stocky Elf, dressed in greys and blues, stepped forward before the dais of Gwyn-ap-Nudd. He gave the King a low bow and began to speak. To Peter and Sarah's great surprise, his report was entirely in verse.

"Under sea, over sea.
Where the crabs crawl,
Where seals play in the lea,
I watch over all!

Fishes swim, shoals flee,
Where nets are cast.
Sardines and sharks I see
Caught in them fast.

Over sea, under sea,
Nothing is sure.
Seals play in the lea,
I see no more."

"Thank you, Eidyol," said the Lord Gwyn.

The Elf stepped away from the dais, bowed once more and returned to his place. The image of the monster from the deep raised its ugly head again in both Sarah and Peter's thoughts. They gave each other a sideways glance simultaneously.

"But there is something wrong in the sea!" they wanted to call out.

But they were prevented, as another Elf came up to the dais to give his report. This Elf was tall and willowy, his clothes the colour of woods in summer.

"I bet he watches the forests," thought Peter. The tall, willowy Elf began to sing in a soft lilting voice:

"Green mist,
Sun kissed
Spreads through our trees.
Bluebells
And Primroses
Aim but to please.
Only the rabbit stirs
The thrush and the vole,
In nodding daffodils, flights of wild bees.
Nothing to trouble
My Lords under Hill,
Nothing but peace, from forest to seas.
All is calm,
All is quiet.
Still times to treasure and seize.
News from afar,
Strange happenings abroad
Serve only to tease.

The calm, peaceful,
Quiet forest
Alone is what one sees!"

"Our thanks to you Eiddyl," smiled Gwyn-ap-Nudd, as he nodded his approval and turned to whisper something to Ederyn who was sitting on his left.

The second Elf returned to his place. So far, the keen eyed Elves had not noticed anything awry. Peter looked round at the assembly and stifled a yawn.

"How many more reports are there going to be?" he wondered. Then there appeared an Elf dressed from head to foot in varying shades of purple and grey.

"He must guard and watch the mountains," thought Sarah. Aunt Myf was distracted. She was watching Catrin and Dylan playing with their toes.

The third Elf spoke gruffly, not in the lilting, pleasant tones of the first two.

"From dizzy heights
On mountains tall,
I view all.

To buzzards black
Who from clouds fall
I do call.

The news they bring
I tell to this Hall,
Though it appaul.

The TROYNT, it comes!
In smoky pall
And fire ball.

In Caerfryddyn where
Both man and beast to maul,
It has the gall!

O Lord of this Hall
To you we call,
Help, or we fall!"

The Elf did not return to his place. He appeared to be waiting for Gwyn-ap-Nudd to speak. All eyes turned to the Lord of the Ellyllon. Gwyn seemed deep in thought. Then, all of a sudden, he ran from his seat on the dais, down the steps to the Elf of the mountains.

"We thank you, friend Ewin, for your sharp eyes and the keen eyes of your buzzards."

Here the Lord Gwyn embraced the Elf of the Mountains heartily. All assembled broke out into a spontaneous round of applause. The Elf whispered something to Gwyn, who embraced him once more, then they parted and returned to their seats.

After this, the Council heard several more Elves from outlying districts give their reports. Then, finally, Gwyn-ap-Nudd looked round at his people. The Hall fell silent, waiting for the next dispatch.

"I call upon Peter and Sarah," the Lord Gwyn said very loudly and looked straight at them both.

The two children jumped about a mile in their seats. They had drifted away into their own thoughts while the Elves had been listening to the various accounts.

"Who will tell their tale first?" Gwyn asked.

Peter went the colour of ripe tomatoes and stood up. It was his duty, he thought, to be the first, if not the only informant. He was the eldest of the Jones children after all! Looking down at Sarah, he could see that he had done the right thing, as she wore a look of extreme relief.

With great discomfort, Peter told the assembly of Elves everything that had happened in Cornwall, beginning with Sarah's dream and their shared vision of the beast from the sea. Once he had begun to tell their story, Sarah was happy to add the odd detail from time to time. Things she remembered better than he.

Gwyn seemed especially interested in Peter's description of the beast, the one that had been given to him by Kevin of the Sympathetic Earth Movement. The Lord Gwyn, Ederyn and Anir all looked extremely concerned. When Peter told them how he had felt on visiting the Stone Circle, Gwyn and Ederyn frowned at each other and whispered something to Anir.

When Peter's tale was told, having finished at the point where Sarah had fainted during the attempt at sending a thought message, the Lord Gwyn got up from his throne. He went to stand at the front of the dais and held up his hand. The Council, who had begun to whisper to each other were silenced. In ringing tones, the Elf Lord enquired of them if there were any further reports to be made. No-one moved. Anir coughed loudly and Gwyn looked round at him.

"Do you have something to add, friend Anir?" Gwyn asked and at once Anir stood up.

"I have just remembered one of the old rhymes that my Mother used to tell me. I don't know if it has any bearing on this meeting or not, but if you wish to hear it..."

He looked at Gwyn for a sign to continue. Gwyn nodded his consent and resumed his seat. Anir cleared his throat and began:

"There is a power in the Old Stones yet,
The way they were hewn,
The way they were set,
Even though folk through the ages forget;
There IS a power in the Old Stones yet.

There is a power in the Old Stones yet,
When the right hand
With the right time is met.
Then power will flow without hindrance or let,
For there is a power in the Old Stones yet.

There is a power in the Old Stones yet,
By sun or by moon,
So easy to get!
It pervades the whole world without fear or fret.
Yes, there is a power in the Old Stones yet!"

Without adding further comment to the rhyme, Anir went to sit down again. Gwyn and Ederyn seemed lost in thought but Sarah wondered if they were actually silent or communicating with each other by thought alone. At last, Gwyn sat up and rang the bell that stood upon a table nearby. Then he addressed the company:

"Friends! We have heard all the reports and they shall be considered at length later today. For the present, I am aware that this meeting has run on well past the Dinner hour. Therefore, I summon the bearers of food and drink to enter the Hall now! My apologies to you all for a longer than usual wait. I am sure you will do justice to the meal as I think all our appetites have been sharpened during the course of this meeting. Enter you bearers!"

A veritable procession of Elves carrying everything from roasts to desserts entered the Great Hall. Peter was particularly glad to

93

see them. The giving of his report had sharpened his appetite no end!

As usual, dinner was a long drawn out affair. Catrin and Dylan had to be taken out, long before it was completely over, by Aunt Myf and Aneryn. Sarah had wondered what Catrin would find to do while she and Peter, and possibly Aunt Myf were busy with the Elves' business. Gwyn and Anir having indicated over dinner that the visitors would be summoned to a more private meeting after the meal was finished.

"Do not worry, the babies have their nursery near to the rooms that we keep set apart for the sick. The lady Morvith and her niece, Eirwen, will care for them today," and Ederyn smiled a merry smile at Sarah. "You may visit them later, if you wish."

An icy tingle crept down Sarah's spine. It was most disconcerting sometimes, to have one's thoughts read in this way.

At length, the whole company of Elves began to drift away from the Great Hall as they finished eating. The Lord Gwyn-ap-Nudd was continuing a low, whispered conversation with Ederyn and Anir. Peter and Sarah felt a little left out. When most of the Elves had gone, Gwyn rose to leave. Ederyn and Anir followed with Peter and Sarah trailing behind them.

"What now?" they thought.

A little way out from the Hall, Anir suddenly walked away in another direction. Nobody told Peter or Sarah what to do, so they continued to follow Ederyn, whose conversation with Gwyn was becoming more and more animated. Sarah gathered from it that there was some kind of disagreement between them as to how to deal with the Troynt. This did not inspire in her the greatest confidence.

"If they don't know what to do about it, then what chance do we have, or anyone else for that matter!" she thought.

Down the tunnels they continued all four, until the massive carved wooden doors of the Room of the Stone of Gardar appeared before them. Gwyn-ap-Nudd pushed on them and they swung open easily. Once again, Peter and Sarah gazed in awe at the carvings and the gold within this most wonderful of rooms that was home to the Elves' miraculous stone.

The Lord Gwyn went at once to the niche where the Stone was held. The light around it flickered and appeared to Peter to be brighter all of a sudden. However, he did not have time to wonder why this was, for at that moment Anir came hurriedly through the doors with Aunt Myf. Ederyn went to the side of the room and brought out a small, richly carved table. This he set up on the dais where lay the golden throne of Gwyn. The Lord Gwyn withdrew the Stone of Gardar from the niche and put it on the table. Then he sat down in his throne. Anir brought stools for the rest of the party and signed to Aunt Myf and the children to be seated.

The Lord Gwyn sat as still as the Stone upon the table, his eyes tight shut. Suddenly, the Elves who had brought the first three reports to the Council came into the Room of the Stone. The last of them, Ewin, was carrying a large roll of parchment. Gwyn-ap-Nudd broke the seal upon it, unrolled it and spread it out. It was a map.

The Gardar Stone was placed at the centre of the map.

"Thus may the Power of The Stone, the blessings of those who dwell beneath the Summer Stars and the Power of all Powers be in our deliberations," said the Elf King.

So the second meeting began. Peter and Sarah studied the map in front of them. It must have been incredibly old, because it looked burnt in several places and the parchment was generally very yellowed, almost brown in fact.

Gwyn, Ederyn and Anir stared hard at the map as if they would like to bore a hole in it with their eyes. The other Elves stood to one side of the table. Aunt Myf was trying hard to stifle a yawn. The large lunch had proved heavier than she expected and she felt very much disposed to sleep.

Sarah thought that she might recognise some of the places on the map. It appeared to show most of the western half of Britain, but some of the names were very odd and completely strange to Sarah and Peter. Gwyn-ap-Nudd began to trace a path with his right finger from Cornwall, up the Severn Estuary and into Wales. He glanced at Peter, who was trying to make sense of the whole thing, and failing dismally.

"Not much like your modern maps, is it!" he said, a merry twinkle in his eye. Peter thought of Father's 'one inch to the mile' maps at home and the Road Atlas.

"Not much," he answered.

"Look, Ederyn," Gwyn seemed suddenly to be enthused over some recollection or another.

"Cornwall, Severn, Caerfryddyn, Tywi, Ceredigiawn, Aber Teifi and we know what should follow, don't we Ederyn!" Ederyn then took up the recitation of names:

"Yes: Aber Teifi, Cwm Cerwyn, Nevern, Prescelly, that is as far as I remember it."

"You ought to remember it is not that long ago, only about 1,500 years, that's all. It might be yesterday!"

Sarah looked up in surprise. Peter continued to stare at the map. He still did not understand any of it.

"Yes, Yes," said Gwyn excitedly, "I am certainly convinced now, especially after the reports we have heard, the Watchers in particular. That of our Guardian also."

Here Anir got up and bowed to Gwyn.

"And Peter of course."

Peter looked up at him.

"Your report was especially important for the description you gathered from that man Kevin, the one from the 'Pathetic Earth Movement',"

"Sympathetic Earth Movement,"

"Quite so, Peter, quite so."

"Then you know what this beast is?" Sarah interrupted.

"Absolutely! Ederyn and I suspected from the very first. That is why we sent Ederyn down to Cornwall at once, the very moment we received your thought message. Your vision, Sarah, was very clear."

"And I was right to go," said Ederyn, "The Troynt, or Twrch Trwyth as it used to be known, was enough of a nuisance before when it took the shape of a boar. This time its power has obviously been potentiated by the use of the power in the Stone Circle."

"Indeed, Anir's rhyme has more than a grain of truth in it," added Gwyn.

"Thank you, my Lord," Anir smiled.

"But why is the beast here now and why is it retracing its journey of long ago?" Gwyn-ap-Nudd asked himself under his breath.

Once again, he drew a track over the ancient map, following a path that had once obviously been familiar to him.

"If we can recall ALL the places that the Troynt went to last time, then we might be able to head it off. If it gets to Prescelly Top, there's no knowing what it might do! We may not be able to stop it," remarked Ederyn coldly, "what do you say Ewin?"

"My Lord, you speak true," said Ewin, "Though I was but a young Elf at the time. Only one hundred and thirty summers, but I remember how the Troynt's power grew phenomenally once he reached Foel Cwm Cerwyn, how could we forget?!"

The other Elves nodded in agreement.

"What do you say Eiddyl and Eidyol?" asked Ederyn.

"A boar it was before. Now it appears in its ancient shape. I say it must be crushed at all costs," said the Watcher of the sea, Eidyol.

"That may be easier said than done!" returned the other, with a stern smile, "however, I have no wish to see this THING trample and burn every forest in Dafydd, Ceredigiawn and Caerfryddyn."

"We might try burying it under a mountain, as we did with that pest, Arddu," said Ewin.

"Hmm," The Lord Gwyn looked thoughtful.

Peter and Sarah could see that he was giving this last solution his careful consideration. Everyone waited, holding their breath.

"Yes," he cried at length, "and no."

This was puzzling.

"What do you mean, my Lord," asked Anir.

"I mean that, 'Yes' it is a good idea to imprison the Troynt under a mountain, and 'No' because I do not think it wise to put it under Foel Cwm Cerwyn. We let Arddu stay there, and look what happened!"

All in the room agreed, for they knew what had happened only too well.

"It might be a good temporary solution," Ederyn suggested.

"It might only last a thousand years, two at most," said Gwyn, "Arthur chased it into the sea at Cornwall:

There let it rot until the World's End!" he said, we were all there, and that is exactly what he said."

"I remember that Merlin was not in agreement with putting the Troynt into the sea."

"No, that is quite true Ederyn and to be quite honest, neither was I. But Arthur was most anxious to return to Gelli Wick and his Gwynhyvar. Two sons he had: Lacheu of the golden hair and Gwydre. After the hunting of the Troynt, or Twrch Trwyth as we called it then, Arthur had only one son. The Troynt slew Gwydre on Cwm Cerwyn. I forgave Arthur everything then, for it goes hard for a parent to bury a child. No-one should have to suffer that! Then too, I feel sure that because the Troynt was in the shape of a boar at the time, most of Arthur's warriors had forgotten what they were dealing with by the end of the chase. They began to think that it was just an overgrown pig that they were hunting, not the shape shifting devil that it really is."

Aunt Myf stirred in her seat. Sarah looked round at her.

"Lord Gwyn," Aunt Myf began, "as a former member of the local Celtic History Society, this story begins to sound familiar. I think I may have read of this chase in a book somewhere. I am sure if I think for a minute it will come to me. I have to say, I am sure that I have seen some of the names on your map before today. Yes, it is coming back!

A strange mixture of a story it was: suitors wanting to marry young maidens and being forbidden to do so. Excuse me, my Lord, but did you not at some stage in the hunt, tell the Emperor Arthur that you did not know where the Troynt was?"

Aunt Myf was not above asking the most awkward questions. Peter and Sarah felt so embarrassed. Why, oh why, did grown-ups have to cause embarrassment at every turn? Peter looked at the floor. Sarah looked at the map, trying to pretend that she did not hear what Aunt Myf was saying.

"You have the advantage of me, Myfanwy," replied Lord Gwyn. "Yes it is true that I said that to Arthur. I was feeling hurt. I had been courting a Lady, as I think Merlin has mentioned to you once before... and there was no reasonable conclusion to my suit, for she had another and could not choose between us. Arthur decreed, therefore, that both of us should fight for the honour of her hand. She was a ward of the Court, you see. Why, I do not know; but then, at that time, she had not revealed her true identity.

The trouble was that we were so well matched that neither of us could gain the upper hand in combat, so it was agreed that we should try again every year at the same time, until one of us should wear the other down. A most unsatisfactory ending, though perhaps it was a good thing that I never did win... So you can see why I was possibly just a touch unhelpful. But I did not tell a lie, though, for at the time I did *not* know the exact whereabouts of the Troynt."

"Humph!" said Aunt Myf, registering her disapproval.

Gwyn's last remark sounded like splitting hairs.

"I do wish that WE knew exactly where it was right now," said Anir loudly, bringing the discussion back to the business in hand. "From what you all say, I gather three things: One, that the Troynt, or Twrch Trwyth or whatever it is, needs to be found. Two, that the Troynt must be un-empowered and three, that it must be locked up somewhere that is permanent, or as permanent as possible. Am I not right, Lord Gwyn?"

Gwyn and Ederyn both looked at Anir but did not reply immediately. Then, after a second or so, Ederyn said:

"Your summing up of the situation is correct, friend Anir. We will now put our minds to trapping the Troynt. As to how it can be un-empowered, that is easy."

Sarah looked up at Ederyn in surprise. She had thought that un-empowering would be that most difficult part of the whole exercise.

"Quite easy," Ederyn repeated. "All that one has to do is to lure the Troynt into another Stone Circle at the right time, etcetera, and it will lose what it gained in the first place."

"And no fried dogs?" asked Peter.

"No fried dogs this time," said Ederyn firmly, "but much thought must be taken as to where it is to be imprisoned. It must be secure," said the Elf.

"Aye," said Gwyn, "or it will be along to bother us again, and we can do without this kind of trouble every other millennium."

"Absolutely!" agreed the Watchers all together.

"Any suggestions, then?" asked Anir.

"There is that big hill in Ireland," said Ewin slowly, "but I don't know if your Kindred, Lord Gwyn, would be willing to take the Troynt over there."

"But that is an excellent idea, Ewin!" returned Gwyn, "I will send messengers to them to sort out details at once, after a preliminary thought message, of course. The Troynt seems to have enjoyed living in the sea, so let us put it under a mountain for a change."

"There are standing stones at Manorbier, I'm sure," said Eidyol, "we might drive it down there perhaps."

"Yes," said Ederyn, "perhaps, although that may prove too far away. We shall look around and see if there is not a nearer circle."

"We know the Troynt is in, or has been in, the Caerfryddyn area," said Eiddyl. "Surely, if you think the Troynt is retracing its steps, you only have to look at the next place on the map."

"That is logical," said Gwyn.

"Will you need Sarah and I any further, Lord Gwyn?" asked Peter.

"No, save perhaps as onlookers only. This is Elves' business, young man. I am sure you have better things to think do at home, Peter. You would not enjoy chasing after this Troynt night after night... much too onerous, if not positively boring I'm sure, for such as you are. I am sure you would not consider it much of *a trial.*"

Gwyn gave Peter his reply in a rather unusually severe fashion; so much so, that it caused Peter to wonder. He thought the remark very odd. Gwyn had mentioned the word *trial* again. He also noticed the blink, or half wink that Gwyn gave then to The

Guardian. Anir smiled knowingly. Was it the hint of yet another **Test?** Peter drew a deep breath. He must be ready for anything he knew, as he had managed to flunk the last one. He must *not* fail again!

The Lord Gwyn continued:

"I am sure your Aunt will agree. You have done very well already by bringing us invaluable information. I am only sorry that this business has caused Sarah so much distress."

Gwyn looked then at Sarah and smiled at her in the most charming manner.

"I am quite well now, thank you," Sarah smiled back at him.

"We are decided, then," declared the Elf King.

"We are!" replied they all.

And so and thus was the meeting in the Room of the Stone ended. The Lord Gwyn-ap-Nudd replaced the Stone of Gardar in its niche. Ederyn picked up the ancient map, doubtless in order to study it further. He left directly with Anir. The three Watchers bowed to Gwyn and also departed. Aunt Myf pulled Peter and Sarah by the arm.

"With your permission, My Lord, we shall leave you to your thoughts. This has been a long day for us all and I must get Catrin home."

"Our thanks to you once again, Myfanwy, Peter, Sarah. This is indeed a weighty matter and requires a great deal of thought. I wish you all a safe journey home and we shall hope to meet once more in Arx Emain when we have tamed this beast once and for all. Farewell!"

Gwyn waved them away and the three visitors left the Golden Room.

"Phew!" said Peter, once they were in the corridor. "Now that was very interesting."

"But did you understand it all?" Sarah asked him, as they went along the tunnel, looking out for the babies nursery.

"Not all of it," replied Peter, "But I'll tell you something..."
He whispered this quietly to Sarah.

"What?" said Sarah, looking at Aunt Myf, who was walking quickly along ahead of them, anxious to collect Catrin.

"Well, maybe I have my own thoughts as to who ought to be hunting the Troynt."

"Oh Peter!"

"I can't be left out of it all," he thought, as he passed quickly up the tunnel. "Supposing this is a Test? What am I supposed to do?" he stopped in the middle of the tunnel to frown and mutter with frustration.

Then Peter stomped off after Aunt Myf who was about to disappear round a bend. Sarah trotted along behind her brother, shaking her head, for she could not imagine what might be going to happen next.

CHAPTER SEVEN

Eirwen

The Babies Nursery was bathed in soft lamp light, with the occasional glow-worm on a shelf for added effect. The walls were carved with every kind of baby creature.

"Ah, Sweet," said Aunt Myf, as she entered the nursery and saw Catrin asleep in a cot.

Dylan was awake and holding his baby arms out to Aneryn, who had just entered the room. She swept him up and thanked Morvith for looking after him.

A young Elf girl came into the nursery behind Aneryn. She had brought a cup of juice for Catrin. She smiled the most wonderful smile at the young visitor, who was beginning to stir. Peter stood in the doorway with Sarah. He had been frowning; puzzled that Anir and the Elves were seeming to shun him. They *must* all know that he desperately wanted to join in the hunt for the Troynt and he did not know at this particular moment if he was meant to do so too, or not!

Then Eirwen turned to greet him and Sarah. They felt slightly shy and so shook hands with her. She must have been very young, for an Elf, for she was only about the same height as Peter. Sarah smiled back at her at once. The thought occurred to her that it was within the realms of possibility that they might be the same age.

"Hello," said Sarah, "I don't think we've met before."

"No," answered Eirwen, "I have been brought here from the North Kingdom. I have come to help my Mother's sister, Morvith, for a while. I am to help her with her duties."

Eirwen smiled her most winning smile at Peter.

"Girls!" he thought, and nearly treated her to a scowl and a frown, but he thought better of it and settled for a half grin instead.

"I hope we meet again," said the Elf maid, "there are never many young Elves around. We do not need to replace ourselves as often or as quickly as you menfolk do. Among my people I am considered to be a baby still."

She lowered her blue eyes to the floor and stuck her bottom lip out in a pout. Then she raised her eyes again to look Peter directly in the face:

"But babies like to have some fun sometimes!" she said, looking from Peter to Sarah. "Would you visit me here, now and again? Duty can be dull, you know."

Her look was so enchanting that suddenly, unexpectedly, Peter's heart warmed to the Elf maid. In doing so he blushed the reddest red ever! Fortunately, Sarah was looking at Eirwen and did not notice, but the Elf maid did, and smiled charmingly at Peter again.

"Of course we'll visit you," Sarah replied warmly, "as long as our holiday lasts. It will be more difficult after this week, though. We have a duty too, it's called school and we have to go to it every day."

At that moment, Morvith called Eirwen to her. Catrin had finished her drink. Eirwen was bidden to remove the used cup and wash it up. Aunt Myf had been talking to Aneryn all the while, as each of them cuddled their baby.

"Dylan has made a friend. It is good," Aneryn said, as she made her way out of the door of the nursery.

"I would love to stay longer, but it is getting late and I must go and prepare our tea at home. It has been a very interesting and rewarding day. Thank you for your hospitality, Aneryn, Morvith, and all of our thanks to the Lord Gwyn. Now then Peter and Sarah, are you ready?"

"Yes, Aunty," answered the two children, Sarah with a touch of resignation; but Peter suddenly found himself more than unwilling to leave.

"Then it's time to go. Goodbye to you Aneryn and Morvith."

Peter and Sarah joined in:

"Goodbye Morvith, goodbye Aneryn."

Aneryn made Dylan wave at them and left. Morvith gave Peter and Sarah a hug. They were old friends by now. Then she kissed Catrin. Anir appeared from round a corner to lead them back to the front gate.

"It feels as if we have hardly been here at all, though we must have been here for hours," Sarah remarked as they prepared to ride out of Arx Emain and back to the road and Aunt Myf's car.

"Like a dream," said Aunt Myf.

"Like going home after an extra specially good holiday," said Peter.

"Come, friends, let us ride," said Anir. The front gate of Arx Emain swung open and hooves that at one moment clattered on stone were soon thudding over the rough terrain of the Pembroke countryside.

When they arrived at the car, all bade fond farewells to Anir.

"You will let us know what happens to the beast, won't you," said Sarah, who was only too happy to leave the problem of the Troynt to the Elves!

"I think for a while at least you will gain more information from your local newspapers!" said Anir with a laugh. "I am sure, however that it will not be long before we meet again, farewell."

Then he said to Peter:

"Chin up. Perhaps you will survive without joining in our wars and woes this once, or maybe not... think it over, choose *right*. These are **testing times!**"

He winked heavily at Peter, then waved at them all, spurred his horse onto a trot and rode away, the borrowed mounts following behind.

The children were soon strapped into the car. Aunt Myf turned on the engine, the radio and then the windscreen wipers, by mistake. In no time at all it seemed, they were back in Newport having tea.

"And just in time too!" declared aunt Myf, as she handed round the plate of cakes. The Bank Holiday weather had taken a turn for the worse and spots of rain began to dribble down the kitchen window. The hills behind Newport looked dark and forbidding under the lowering sky. Peter and Sarah were glad to be snug indoors. Aunt Myf put on the light.

"That's better," she said, "much cosier. More Teisen Lap, anyone?"

A quiet night followed the excitement of the day. Uncle Tomos arrived home late for supper. He was not in a good mood. Aunt Myf did her best to ease his burden but the trouble seemed immovable and mostly concerned with a letter sent by County HQ at the last minute. Right at the end of the afternoon.

"Just finishing my tea and biscuits and this letter arrives on my desk!" he said.

"What was it all about, Dearest," Aunt Myf asked him.

"It was all about this arsonist everyone is complaining about. We all though that it was an English phenomenon, but now he seems to be operating here in Wales!"

"Perhaps there are two of them," said Aunt Myf, furiously stirring the tea in the pot with the sugar spoon.

"Two what, dear?"

"Two arsonists. Perhaps the fires in Wales belong to some copy cat criminal."

"I suppose you could be right," Uncle Tomos thought about it for a few seconds. Then he said: "Doesn't matter really. If the arsonist strikes anywhere near here we shall have to get the whole Force out, stake-outs and everything."

"Golly," exclaimed Peter.

"How exciting!" said Sarah.

"Not at all," replied Uncle Tomos. "It will mean sleepless nights and sitting around in all sorts of uncomfortable places, waiting for the criminal to strike. We have our forensic team working on a psychological profile already."

"Much help THAT will be on the Troynt!" thought Peter.

Uncle Tomos continued his complaints, while Aunt Myf listened attentively and 'tut-tutted' in all the right places.

Peter's face drew up once more into a frown as he thought over how the Lords of Arx Emain had seemingly cast him off. Or had they? He began to think it over.

"What did Gwyn mean by that wink he gave to Anir?" he muttered under his breath, "and what did that wink of Anir's mean also? What am I supposed to understand from them?" Peter thought and thought. He shook his head, trying to work it all out, unaware that Sarah was watching him.

"After all, I *did* give them tons of information. Gwyn must have asked me at least half a dozen times about what happened when we got to the Stone Circle, and twenty times about that Kevin's description of the Troynt."

Peter put his head in his hands and went over and over again, everything that had happened during the meeting at Arx Emain. Was the wink and the tone that Gwyn had used to him at the end of the meeting a signal? *Was* he being tested again? *Were* the Elves inviting him to join the hunt after all? But how could he get himself involved in the hunt for the beast again? It *must* be the start of another Test. Gwyn had definitely mentioned a trial. He thought and thought. At the end of their visit; hadn't Anir said something about **testing times**...

"That's it!" he thought, but how was he to get more information upon what to do next?

After several minutes, Sarah noticed a slow smile spread across his face. She said to herself immediately:

"He's had an idea!"

After that, she could not wait for supper to finish and Aunt Myf, Catrin and Uncle Tomos to disappear up stairs for Catrin's bath time. When they finally did so, Sarah caught Peter, pushed him on to the sofa and pummelled him with both fists until he swore that he would *give in* and tell all.

"Ouch! Not so hard, little Sis! You are getting heavier than you were. I'll tell all, I swear. Just get off me will you, and let me breathe."

Sarah did as he asked, having remarked that she thought Peter was a rat.

"I know you have an idea, why couldn't you tell me about it earlier?"

"I couldn't."

"Well, you might at least have whispered something to give me a hint while we cleared the supper things away."

"No, I could not! It is far too complicated."

Peter assumed an air of magnificent superiority. Sarah hit him over the head with a cushion.

"Well jolly well tell me now, OR ELSE!"

Peter made himself comfortable on the sofa and gave Sarah a space to sit on.

"Ready?" he asked, only he wasn't really.

"Ready!"

"You have to understand, Sis, that I haven't worked out all the details yet and it might not actually work out, but here's the bare bones of it. In the first place it has to involve Eirwen."

"Eirwen!? Are you quite mad?"

Sarah could not work it out. Usually her brother was inclined to distance himself from girls of any sort.

"I thought you didn't like playing with girls?"

"I didn't say anything about playing. This is deadly serious!"

"So what's the plan?"

"Listen: I, we, can contact Eirwen in the usual way."

"By thought message?"

"Yes, of course by thought message. We'll tell her to meet us somewhere near here. I'm sure she'll come. I think she would like something to do that brings her out of Arx Emain. She did say that she would like some fun. Perhaps we could ask her to meet us up on Carn Ingli."

Peter's voice trailed off into silence. He was away, deep in thought, working out his master plan. Somehow, he had to come up with something brilliant. So far, he thought that if he contacted Eirwen, she might also bring with her someone who

110

might kindly explain to the puzzled Peter what he must do next about The Test!

"So...?" Sarah said again, nudging him with her elbow.

"Sorry, yes, where was I?"

"Up on Carn Ingli Common with Eirwen."

"Oh yes, OK then... Eirwen meets us and brings that old map of Gwyn's with her."

That was IT! If he asked her to bring the map to him, *someone else* with the appropriate seniority must surely have to accompany her. Someone who might be able to tell him what to do. However, he did not tell Sarah everything for the moment. The Tests, his ambition to be Guardian, or even apprenticed to Anir in some small way, was a deep and deadly secret thus far.

"What!" cried Sarah, "wouldn't that be frightfully dangerous? Ederyn or Gwyn would be bound to miss it and Eirwen would get into loads of trouble, AND so would we! They'd be super angry."

"OK, a copy then, or I could make a copy," Peter stammered. "Then we could all study it, decide where the Troynt is going next and follow it. Perhaps we could even lead it to a place where we could do all that un-empowering. Then Gwyn can take it and put it under the mountain in Ireland. Happy ending and everyone satisfied."

This last part of the plan was ridiculous, he knew; but with the first part, Peter was satisfied. His plan to get hold of a senior member of Arx Emain must succeed!

"I think you have gone completely off your brain!" said Sarah, who was less than happy with Peter's plan. "Supposing something goes wrong?" she asked, "suppose the Elves find out you've got their map? And remember, Anir said that the Troynt eats ANYTHING! I don't fancy ending up as its fried dinner."

Having thought about the master plan, Sarah began to be suspicious about Peter's motives. The plan seemed to have less to do with logical tactics and more to do with getting Eirwen out of Arx Emain. Why should he want to do that?

"And," she said sharply, "we mustn't get Uncle Tomos fried either. If he or any of the Policemen go anywhere near that thing, they will get fried, sure as anything!"

"I'm going to try it, though, Sis. Are you with me?"

"I'll sleep on it. I might let you know in the morning. I can hear Catrin is out of the bath now and I'm next, 'cos I'm tired. Look, there's Uncle Tomos coming downstairs and off to his study. I'm going up now, coming Peter?" and light-footedly, Sarah tiptoed up the stairs to prepare for bed.

Peter remained on the sofa. He knew that his master plan was incomplete. It would have to worked on and he decided to spend the rest of the evening doing precisely that. However, first things first, he must contact Eirwen and that must be done this very night. No telling Sarah though. He would let her go to sleep before he made any move at all.

"I can't risk frightening her again," he thought, remembering the fainting fit at Falmouth. He also did not want her to know all his reasons for meeting Eirwen on Carn Ingli. That settled, Peter made his way upstairs to join Sarah in preparations for bed time.

Next morning, news arrived from Mother and Father in the form of an airmail letter.

"Good news?" enquired Aunt Myf, as she brought in the toast and put it down on the breakfast table.

"Yes thank you," said Sarah, scanning the lines.

"Dearest Peter and Sarah," the letter began, "the conference is going splendidly. Your father has presented two papers already, one on Rome and one on his recent finds in Greece..."

Sarah read on quickly. The rest of the letter described the Hotel where their parents were staying, the town, the people at the conference, a coach trip to see Moorish ruins, and a local excavation. Sarah's lip began to wobble. She did not like Mother and Father being abroad without her. By the time she arrived at:

"Lots and lots of love and kisses..."

A tear had plopped into her tea. Just at that moment, however, a squawk from Peter soon diverted her attention to the bad news of the day. It was what everyone had been dreading. The Troynt had reached Cardigan!

Peter read the grim headlines.

"BARN FIRE AT FARM CLOSE TO WILD LIFE PARK! FEARS FOR LIVESTOCK!"

Peter read on aloud:

"Whole heard of cows feared slaughtered. Tons of hay gone up in flames."

Sarah gasped. The Troynt was certainly becoming greedier. What else might it consume?

"That's me off to the Station!" sighed Uncle Tomos, wiping the egg and bacon from his mouth and looking round for his briefcase. "I'll let you know Myfanwy, if I have to stay away tonight. With a bit of luck I might get my Sergeant to do most of the donkey work, but we'll have to see. That letter I got from HQ yesterday says that the Chief expects results and he expects them as of yesterday! I must get my brain going. Expect me when you see me. Have a good day all!" and grabbing a hasty last piece of toast, he left for the front door and the car and a heavy day at the Constabulary.

"Will Uncle Tomos have to be on the stake-out?" asked Sarah with concern.

"Not necessarily dear; he might have to stay in the Police Station all night, though, to co-ordinate the whole exercise." Aunt Myf finished feeding soggy Cornflakes to Catrin and went to fetch her an egg.

"Boy beg?" Catrin said triumphantly.

"Yes darling, 'Boy beg'. Now eat up, there's a good girl."

Peter and Sarah made their excuses and left their Aunt to her very messy work. Catrin was not very good at wielding a spoon and often had to be helped. They went straight out into the garden and sat on the bench. It was damp from overnight rain. Sarah shivered.

"I think we shall visit Carn Ingli this afternoon," Peter announced.

"Oh yes?"

"Yes, I am sure we will find our friend up there."

"Eirwen, why? Oh Peter, you didn't, without me? How could you!"

"You fell asleep early last night and I didn't want to wake you up."

Peter did not tell her anything else. He was not ready yet to give up any of his secrets.

"Is that all you have to say?"

"For the moment, yes, until we get to Carn Ingli. Then you'll see!"

"I hope your thought message was a good one then. We shall feel such fools, waiting up there if Eirwen doesn't come."

"We shall just have to wait and see if she does come, that's all. Now be a good girl Sarah and leave me to think. I must be sure that I have my plan right."

"Very well, brother dear," said Sarah in the most sarcastic tones, "I shall go and read the papers. See you at lunch."

She left Peter alone to think of his plan, while indicating clearly that she was in a 'huff'.

At lunch, Aunt Myf noticed that Peter and Sarah were both very quiet. She supposed that they might be bored.

"Wouldn't you like a run out in the car?" she offered brightly. Peter cheered up immediately. This was more than he hoped for. Perhaps she was half an Elf and could read his mind too!

"Yes please," he said at once. Then he asked if they could go to Carn Ingli before Aunt Myf had time to think of asking them where they might want to go.

Sarah had decided to remain in her *mood* all afternoon, but now, knowing that going to Carn Ingli was part of Peter's plan, she began to feel quite excited. Having ascertained that an ice cream cornet might also be included as part of the outing, Sarah cheered up also. Aunt Myf felt greatly rewarded by their reception of her plan for the afternoon's entertainment and the car was soon got out. The children were firmly strapped in and Catrin became really excited.

"Ice Cleem!" she exclaimed loudly, having heard it mentioned "Ice Cleem!"

"No, darling, no ice cream just yet," her mother told her, "walk first, then ice cream," Aunt Myf insisted, as she turned off the main road and up to find the car park.

Unfortunately for Aunt Myf, when they arrived, there was an ice cream van IN the car park, taking advantage of the first flush of tourists. She knew that she was beaten and provided everyone with an ice before their walk began.

They made at once for Mynydd Carn Ingli as usual. All along the way Peter thought and hoped, and hoped and thought of Eirwen. Did she know? Would she come? Had she received his thought messages? He plodded steadily on behind Aunt Myf, Catrin and Sarah. Sarah and Aunt Myf were engaged in a conversation about the hill fort and hut circles that lie around the common.

"Please Eirwen, please come and *do* bring somebody else with you," Peter repeated, over and over again.

He was so lost in thought that he was quite surprised when they arrived at the hill fort. Aunt Myf had brought drinks and biscuits with her and she sat down by some of the stones to rest, while sharing out the small picnic. Sarah and Catrin sat down beside her. Peter wandered listlessly round the stones, all the time on the look out for any sign that Eirwen might be there.

The snack was soon over, but Aunt Myf appeared quite content to rest where she was. Sarah played with Catrin. Peter began to wonder if Eirwen had failed to get any of his desperate messages, when a party of riders came up the hill on one of the many bridlepaths. At first they looked like any other band of trekkers. Then, as they drew nearer, Peter nearly fell over in surprise. The foremost rider was waving and waving. It was none other than Eirwen herself.

"What on earth or under it...?" Sarah said to herself, but Peter had jumped up and was waving and waving back.

The party of riders drew up behind the hill fort. Behind Eirwen were: Ewin, Eiddyl, Eidyol *and* Anir. Eirwen jumped down from her pony.

"We got your message," she said, waving a large blue cloth bag in front of Peter's nose. "Here's the map, but you may only borrow it."

Peter was dumbfounded that she had actually brought it. Sarah came running up, followed by Aunt Myf with Catrin.

"This is splendid! But does everyone at Arx Emain know about my plan?" asked Peter, who had not expected to see the Watchers as well as Anir.

"No," Anir assured him, "but if ever you *should* want to be secretive, you would have to be very careful when sending thought messages to Elves."

"Only I got your message," added Eirwen, "but of course I had to tell Anir in order to get the map, and he would not let me come out riding without the Watchers coming too!"

"Well, I think that's only right," said Peter.

His plan was working well so far. Better than he expected in fact, for it had brought Anir himself. Did he guess that the map was just an excuse?

"Now, now, what's all this?" said Aunt Myf, "I thought Gwyn did not want the children to be involved with this anymore?"

"I'm sure that is true, *in the main*," replied Anir, winking at Peter.

Then Anir looked suddenly more serious. He paused as if he were thinking. Then he took Peter by the arm and led him to one side, while Eirwen took the map from the bag and began to show it to Aunt Myf and Sarah. They were fascinated and poured over it eagerly.

"It might prove to make up one of **The Tests**, might it not," said Anir to Peter.

"Might it?" asked Peter, his heart thumping inside his chest with excitement, "Oh, great! I hoped you would tell me what to do next. Is this really another Test?"

"Well, we shall have to wait and see what we shall see," said Anir mysteriously, "all I shall say to you now, Peter, is watch and be vigilant. You will know what to do when the time comes, and I am sure that you will *not* let me down."

He gave Peter a large, knowing wink, as if he expected Peter to understand what he was talking about. Peter felt his stomach jump into his throat, as he felt the thrill of facing another one of the Tests for the Guardianship; or rather perhaps, the Apprenticeship to it. It was also very exciting for him to be fully included in the adventures of the Elves again.

Then Anir brought Peter back to the others and said aloud for all to hear:

"Gwyn and Ederyn and some of the others have gone to see if they can find the Troynt, as it is very close and bound to come this way soon. You may as well look at the map Peter, now we have brought it here, but I do not think it will be of any more help to you than it has to us at Arx Emain."

Eirwen handed Peter the bag, and he took the hint. He withdrew the ancient map from the cloth bag and spread it on the ground. There were so many names on it that he did not understand; Mynydd this and Dyffryn that. Not much to help until the Prescelly Mountain range was shown, where Foel Cwm Cerwyn and the other cairns were marked, Nevern also and Cardigan.

"What was this map for?" Peter asked.

"It is a map marking many things known to our people," said Eirwen, "but the places within it, marked in red, are those that were attacked by the Troynt, or Twrch Trwyth, millennia ago."

"Gosh! Wow!" exclaimed Peter.

"Well, now *you* know; we *all* know," said Anir, "I also know, Gwyn and Ederyn too, that you picked something up when you made contact with the Stone Circle, after the beast was fully released and empowered. It may be, that you are required to handle the Stones again," Anir said.

However, Peter was only half listening to him, as he was thinking hard.

"There is a Stone Circle that I know of very near to Prescelly top," said Peter, looking for it on the strange map.

All looked at him now, giving him their full attention.

"Couldn't the THING be driven into it and its power be undone there?" he said.

"That is almost precisely what Gwyn intends to do. Strange is it not, that you both think the same!" replied Anir, "Gwyn and Ederyn believe that it is holed up by day somewhere near The Devil's Bridge. And comes out at night to feed and destroy all in its path. Goodness knows what it will do if it gets much stronger!"

"It is not far from Aberystwyth, this Devil's Bridge," said Eiddyl, "it is a beautiful place where the river Mynach runs through a deep gorge. The Devil's Bridge rises over a deep cleft in the rocks. The forests are very wonderful there. I do hope they are not burnt."

118

"The Lord Gwyn thinks that the landscape around Devil's Bridge must mimic in some way, the ancestral home of the Troynt," said Ewin.

"Where did it live?" asked Aunt Myf.

"No-one is exactly certain," said Anir, "for the Troynt is immensely old. It is older, perhaps than even the oldest of stories about it. Some of the Elders at Arx Emain insist that he once roamed the lands somewhere around the Cheddar Gorges and other lands about the Severn Estuary. He is after all, a creature of the underworld."

"Then what about *all that* in Arthur's time?" asked Aunt Myf, completely mystified.

"He is like most of THEM, a shape shifter," replied Eidyol. "That is how he could live in the sea."

Sarah shuddered as she remembered her vision of the monster rising from the deep.

"The Emperor Arthur it was, first deprived the Troynt of his lands. It has been biding its time for a revenge attack ever since," said Ewin.

"But when it came out of Cornwall this time, why didn't it stay in the Cheddar Gorge?" asked Peter.

"Because you menfolk have taken the Gorge over!" said Eirwen, and giggled.

Peter and Sarah had both visited the Gorge and could see why the Troynt, a solemn beast of the underworld might not fit in there.

"It cannot go back to its own lands, so it is presently wreaking revenge for the apparent confiscation by tourism of its ancestral home," explained Anir.

"I almost feel sorry for it," said Sarah.

"You wouldn't if you were one of the farmers who has lost all his livestock, all the sheep and cows that have been fried recently," Anir said again, "we must contain it in a safe place soon before it does something really dreadful. Remember, Sarah and Peter, the Troynt will destroy all in its path and it will eat ANYTHING!"

Suddenly, an awful thought occurred to Peter.

"The Pembrokeshire Police Force," he stammered, "they are going after the beast. They think IT is a criminal gang. They may be out after it tonight!!

Aunt Myf went as white as a sheet. "Oh my poor Tomos," she murmured.

Then she looked Anir hard in the face:

"Well, cousin Anir, and what are you going to do about that, hmm? What are you going to do?"

CHAPTER EIGHT

Hunting The Troynt

The party of Elves and Anir departed shortly after further plans had been made with Peter and Sarah... and especially Peter. Peter made a hasty copy of the ancient map in his notebook, really for effect alone, as his plan to bring Anir to him had worked. Anir promised to return to Peter and Sarah with the Watchers, but not necessarily Eirwen, later that evening.

Peter and Sarah, he said, could ride with the Elves who were coming up from Arx Emain in order to assist Gwyn-ap-Nudd, Ederyn and the others with the hunting and imprisoning of the Troynt. Gwyn, Ederyn and a large part of the Elvish Army had gone up to the Gorge of the Mynach River to try and dislodge the beast from its temporary home at Devil's Bridge. The Immortals then hoped to drive it, by one means or another, down to the Prescelly Mountains and from there, right into the Stone Circle. Peter was surprised and delighted to discover that his own plan matched that of the Lord Gwyn's exactly.

"Who thought of it first?" he wondered.

Once they got up on the Prescellys, Peter and Sarah gathered that the Elves were expecting BIG trouble. Any *onlookers* would be expected to keep well out of the way until such time that they were allowed, or asked to make some kind of contribution to the proceedings. BUT, as time went on, Peter gained from The Guardian's many nods and winks, the distinct suspicion that Anir expected Peter to become seriously involved by the end of it all!

Gwyn and Ederyn hoped to drive the Troynt down into the Stone Circle at Gorse Fawr where it might then be disarmed, un-empowered and generally tamed. Then the Lord Gwyn would be able, through the power of the Gardar Stone, to propel the Troynt over to his kindred in Ireland. Once there, the Elves had agreed to place the beast under a huge mound of stones and earth, known there as New Grange. There, hopefully this time, the Troynt would remain beyond knowledge and out of the way of man and Elf kind for ever... or for a considerable length of time at least!

Anir and the Watchers then escorted Eirwen and the map back to Arx Emain. Eirwen protesting all the way back from Carn Ingli that she wanted to witness the downfall of the Troynt. Not only that, but bravely, or foolishly, she said that she wanted to have some part in it all!

Anir told her very forcefully that Morvith, and her Mother and Father in the North Kingdom would not appreciate her being eaten.

"But I only want to have some fun!" Peter and Sarah heard her say.

"She's a bit of a handful, that one," observed Aunt Myf, as she put Catrin in the baby carrier and slung her over her shoulders. "They'll have to watch that Eirwen, mark my words if they don't!" she said, setting off at a smart pace back along the track to the car park.

Once safely back at home, a council of war was held immediately over tea. Aunt Myf agreed, unwillingly it must be said, that Sarah and Peter might be *onlookers* in the hunt for the Troynt. Privately she thought that they might also keep an eye on her unsuspecting and unsuspicious husband. If only he might be kept away from the ravenous beast!

"But that is all! I wouldn't like to have to tell your Mother and Father that you had been devoured while they were away. What sort of Aunt would I be? Tell me that!"

She was quite adamant that the children's safety must come above everything else, and Peter and Sarah promised most faithfully that they would behave themselves.

"I do wonder about that Eirwen, though," Aunt Myf went on, "how will she behave?"

This was a continual worry to her for the rest of the evening.

Uncle Tomos rang at seven o'clock to say the he would be staying over night at the Constabulary.

"I might even have to go up to Cardigan," he said, "things are hotting up, if you'll forgive the pun!"

Aunt Myf did not find Tomos' little joke at all funny. She told him to be very, very careful and to keep away from any fires.

"Oh my poor Tomos," was all she could say for some time afterwards.

Catrin was already in bed. Peter and Sarah got ready for bed and lay down in the guest room, as they did not know exactly when Anir would come.

Sarah fell asleep. Peter lay on his back, the map for once crystal clear in his mind. Was the next place on the list really the Cairns on the Prescelly Mountains? Would Gwyn-ap-Nudd be able to remove the power of the beast, or might it make a break for it and escape... running away to the sea at Porth Cleis? That was the last place on the list of strange names, but the first place that it had appeared in formerly. Porth Cleis was where it had been when it had first come over from Ireland to annoy Arthur and all his warriors.

As he lay on his back, Peter wondered many things that he must ask Anir about sometime, if and when he got the chance. Why had Merlin not been contacted if the beginnings of the trouble lay in his times? Or did they? The Elves had said that the Troynt was incredibly old. However, he and Sarah had immense faith in the wizard's powers. Surely, he could easily dispatch a monster such as this one.

Then too, where was the Ring of Concealment? Peter knew that Anir had custody of it. With that one might sneak up on a beast and take it by surprise. But he knew, even as he thought of it, that Anir rarely used the Ring and at present the Elves seemed to prefer the full frontal attack.

Then he wondered, was Gwyn-ap-Nudd actually going to bring the Gardar Stone out of Arx Emain in order to push the Troynt through its portal? And how DID those Stone Circles work? What technology was it that drove them?

Then, there was the question of the Tests. How was he expected to fulfil the next one to the Elves' satisfaction? And what, exactly, did they want him to do? These, and many other thoughts went round and round in his overactive mind, until at last he too fell asleep.

At half past midnight, a soft knock could be heard on the front door. Horses hooves sounded upon the main road outside Aunt Myf's house. Anir had arrived. Peter was awake at once and up and dressed in a trice. Sarah made all sorts of complaining noises, but as she did not want to be left out of things, she hurried herself and was ready soon after Peter.

Aunt Myf told them for the millionth time to be careful and do exactly what they were told.

"They shall be onlookers only," said Anir, "they shall not take part in the chase tonight," he promised her, as he led the excited pair to where the others were waiting with two spare horses.

"Did you really mean that, about being onlookers only?" Peter asked him.

"For the moment... yes!" replied Anir quite forcefully, so that Peter did not ask him anything more for a while, though noting that he had said: *for the moment*!

The others turned out to be the three Watchers and also Eirwen, with Aneryn who was acting as Eirwen's chaperone. Eirwen had absolutely insisted on coming, so Aneryn said that she must come too.

The eight of them set off at once for Foel Cwm Cerwyn with the greatest of expectations. In one way they were not disappointed. Gwyn-ap-Nudd and Ederyn and about a hundred Elves were already at the peak. They had managed to winkle the Troynt out from its hideout at Devil's Bridge and had successfully driven it down to the Prescelly range of mountains. There, the assembled company were treated to a show of fireworks, such as had never been seen on Prescelly Top before.

Peter and Sarah gathered that it was angry! The Troynt was truly terrifying in its present form. It seemed wrapped in some kind of dark cloud and all that could be seen was a vague shape, as of a horse, but one that had very thin forelegs and a beak instead of a muzzle. When provoked by the Elves, it spat fire.

125

Gwyn and Ederyn, however, did not seem to mind getting it angry. Their steely swords and golden armour shone brightly in the light of the waning moon.

Anir kept his little group as far away as possible from the affray. It became rather like watching a game. Every now and again, they felt that Gwyn, Ederyn and the Elves had scored a point, so they cheered. But every now and again the Troynt scored a point. Indeed, several Elves had been severely singed already. Then the onlookers shouted and heckled the beast, feeling it reasonably safe on the sidelines to do so.

"Boo!" yelled Peter and Sarah. "Go away you beastly Troynt!"

Then all of a sudden , the Troynt must have decided that it had had enough. With a mighty roar, it fled down from the peaks towards Foel Drygarn, that dark and dismal place which had always given Sarah the creeps. Every time the Troynt touched a rock on the ground, which was frequently, as the road between Foel Cwm Cerwyn and Foel Drygarn is littered with rocks like a moonscape, it sent the rock spinning into the air. That would have been bad enough, but it set the rocks alight with a phosphorescent flame which did the pursuing Elves no good at all, as they burnt anyone they fell on grievously.

Gwyn and his small army bravely took up the chase, but it was no good. The Troynt was too quick for them and disappeared off back to its hideout, setting fire to anything that got In its way. This included hay barns, animal pens, a post office and a school hall, not to mention a local W.I. meeting hall and a scout hut.

Gwyn rode back over to Anir when he saw the Troynt disappearing past Crymych on the road to Newcastle Emlyn. Ederyn and the rest would keep on its trail and try to prevent its doing too much damage. Down below them, on the main road, Peter and Sarah could hear sirens. These were the sirens of the Police cars and fire engines that were rushing to attend to the fires set by the monstrous beast.

"Uncle Tomos will be having a busy night," Sarah thought.

"Is all well?" the Lord Gwyn asked Anir.

"So far, but I noticed that you were not able to contain it tonight."

"No, Anir, but we shall. We must! I underestimated the number of troops required. We shall bring more tomorrow. It is a balance that I must strike between catching this pest without drawing too much attention to us all, or completely flooding this whole area with our armies. But we must succeed soon, or you and Ederyn, and I will have to think again. The Troynt is becoming greedy beyond anything we could have imagined and certainly beyond what we all remember of it last time."

"Well my Lord, I suppose it had not tasted warm blood for an age, not for 1,500 years or so I guess. It was bound to be hungry," Aneryn said.

The children and the Watchers remained silent. The Elf King was evidently much wearied. He rode slumped in the saddle. Sarah forgot that they were not supposed to be there.

"I'm sure you will win tomorrow," she said in an effort to cheer him up.

Gwyn smiled at her and sat up just a little taller.

"Thank you Sarah, we must win. If not today or tomorrow then the next day. At any rate, there is no more to be done tonight. Anir, you may take your friends home and the Watchers with Aneryn shall return with us, including the *little one who ought not to be here.*"

Gwyn looked sideways at Eirwen. Peter was sure that she must be blushing under the Elf Lord's stern gaze.

"Come on then, HOME!" said Anir.

He led Peter and Sarah away down the mountain as Gwyn went off in the other direction with the army, back to Arx Emain. The two children were home well before the sun was fully up in the bright morning sky and easily before Uncle Tomos dropped in for a very late breakfast, or was it brunch? Needless to say, he and the rest of the Police had been having a very bad night.

"Couldn't be worse," he said, "and there's no sign of anyone. Not so much as a smell of 'em, and my sergeant Pugh has twisted his ankle, running after one of the pigs that didn't get fried, he was."

"Dear, dear," murmured Aunt Myf sympathetically, and put his eggs and bacon down in front of him.

Uncle Tomos noticed nothing strange at home, except that Peter and Sarah were keen on having late mornings. He himself went to his study for a nap, before returning to the Constabulary where he was to co-ordinate the following night's stake-outs.

"These criminals seem to hit anything between here and Aberystwyth, but in the main, it seems to be centred in this area. We are putting more men on the job tonight. I am afraid I may not be home again until tomorrow, Myfanwy."

Then off he went again, mystified as ever. They gathered that the forensic team had not been awfully successful in coming up with a psychological profile of the suspects!

"Not surprising when you know what it is they are chasing," said Peter, "a great big psychopathic cloud, a horse with a bird's beak that likes fire raising, and which eats..."

"ANYTHING!" Sarah added dismally.

That night the same procedure was followed. At twelve o'clock Anir knocked at the door. The Watchers, Aneryn, Eirwen and the two spare horses were waiting outside the garden gate as before. Everyone was now out on the chase on a semi-official footing. This meant that Gwyn now knew, truly, that they were going. Sarah suspected, however, that he had known all the time. She and Peter both wondered after this if Elves were able to intercept each other's thought messages. They *must* be able to... it was just not logical that they could not.

This night, Anir led them to Nevern. A trail of flames showed where the beast had preceded them. This time Gwyn and Ederyn had a force of two hundred Elves, round about the Prescelly mountains and another one hundred and fifty in and around Nevern. They were expecting a big battle.

Once again, Anir kept his group of observers away from the main centre of action. In fact they were so far away, hiding down the side of the Church, that they did not see much at all. In between the fireworks, Peter found the opportunity to ask Anir the questions that had been bothering him. Anir was pleased to answer him thus:

"We have not contacted Merlin this time because, for one thing, Gwyn-ap-Nudd and his Kindred ought to be able to dispatch this THING before it becomes much stronger. For another, we are fairly certain that Merlin is otherwise engaged. He has made no contact with us for some time, neither has he requested the power of the Stone of Gardar since he repaired to Greece with *that* goddess. Indeed, he may still be on holiday with, *you know who.*"

Peter nodded. The last time that he and Sarah had seen Merlin, he had delivered them all from the wrath of the goddess Demeter. He had then managed to tame her enough to actually accompany her back to Ancient Greece! Perhaps by this time she had 'tamed' Merlin! Peter thought on this for a little. Then he asked Anir if he still kept the Ring of Concealment.

"I do," replied Anir, "though it must remain hidden for the present. Neither I nor anyone else will require its use during these battles with the beast."

"Will Sarah or I be able to use it again?"

"Only at my discretion and only in great need. You, Peter, may not keep it again; or at least, not for a long time. For now you know what it is and what it does. You have grown up a great deal since you had it last. Only The Guardian may keep it. The Oath

129

he has taken and the trials and tests he has endured, ensure that the ring remains in safe hands. Only as **Guardian** may one have this treasure."

Anir's tone was most serious and Peter sensed that he was supposed to take this last comment to heart. He understood that Anir was trying to tell him something about the Guardianship. However, Peter was not able to work out altogether what Anir meant, so he went on to his next question.

"Will Gwyn really bring the Gardar Stone out of Arx Emain? I always thought that the Elves were frightened of losing it again."

"Eh!"

Peter repeated his question. Anir had been momentarily distracted by the amount of flames shooting from off the top of the old castle mound.

"Gwyn must be having a time of it up there," he muttered. "Sorry, Peter, what were you saying?" Peter asked him once more about the Gardar Stone.

"I think Gwyn probably does have it at the ready, so to speak. A quick push through the portal and before the Troynt knows anything about it, Gwyn's kindred will have him out at the other side and buried before you can say *spiral castle.*

"But Anir, how do they know that the beast will get weaker if they trap it in the Stone Circle? And how do the Stone Circles work anyway?"

"I am not exactly sure myself," said Anir, "I only know what my Mother once told me about them. That it is something to do with the particular shape and size of them, also the way in which they have been carved in the first place. The people who made them were very skilled, very skilled indeed. They made the stones to give power. The Circles are energy potentiators. That is to say that they collect certain energies and when they are tuned in, or resonate with each other all together, THAT is when things happen.

The trouble is that most people today have forgotten all the keys that make the Stones work for them. Rather as if you lost all your power stations tomorrow and were unable to work out how to construct them or work them again. The Sympathetic Earthers must have hit on the right key purely by chance, and the Troynt being nearby, it obviously took advantage of the available power supply to become fully active."

"But what I want to know is..." began Sarah, who had been listening to the last few questions and Anir's replies.

"Hmm... Ssh!" Anir put his hand to his lips, signalling silence.

He was trying to pick up the noises coming from the top of the castle mound. They could all see the smoke rising. The start of yet another futile fire.

"I think that we shall withdraw from here. Discretion being the better part of valour, especially with Ladies present. Come, we will go back down the road out of Nevern and across the Afon Nyfer."

"But that means that we shall be on the way back to Newport," protested Peter.

"It does indeed, and by the sound of those sirens, the Police are not far away. I do not think you want to be rounded up as suspects. Just think how embarrassing it would be for your Uncle Tomos! Anyway, the battle is over for tonight. Look, the Lord Gwyn is riding northwards once again. Two nights now he has lost the Troynt. We will have to see if the third night will prove decisive."

Anir led the weary band down the road and away back to Newport. They departed just as the sound of the sirens grew louder and the screech of tyres upon the Nevern road became closer. As they slipped away, Peter thought he heard shouts and the noise of several Police whistles being blown.

"Thank goodness, they haven't managed to catch up with that Troynt, or *Twerp Trick* yet," thought Sarah as her horse trotted on behind Aneryn's pretty grey mare.

It was dawn as they parted from Anir and the Watchers, Eirwen and Aneryn. A sea mist rolled in and swirls of grey mist rose up and the hills behind the town of Newport were lost in cloud. Everything dripped. If it had been cooler, there might have been a hoar frost. Peter and Sarah were glad to get back into bed. They did not wake again until Aunt Myf brought them breakfast in bed with a post card on each tray, propped up by a beautiful, brown, boiled egg.

Peter's postcard was from Emma. It read:

"Dear Peter,
Nothing exactly exciting is going on here now. What is happening with you and the...!? We are simply bursting to know! Write soon. Love Emma."

Sarah's postcard read:

"Dear Sarah,
We are having a wonderful time! We are having great fun doing lots of swimming at the Lido on the hill. The pool even has its own wave machine! I hope you are well. Love from Amy, xx."

They read each other's cards and laughed about the different descriptions of the same holiday. Then Peter got up and went downstairs with Sarah following slowly behind him. They both felt relaxed, but a little nervous and excited also. Would this evening see the final 'push' and the dematerialization of the monster?

Uncle Tomos arrived at twelve for lunch. He was looking very tired indeed.

"I must catch some sleep," he said after lunch, which was lamb chops with vegetables and a chocolate pudding.

Aunt Myf went upstairs to see that the bed was turned down and they left him there for the rest of the afternoon. Aunt Myf wanted to go shopping with Catrin in town and Peter and Sarah went with her. They simply HAD to do something to occupy the time because both of them felt more and more nervous about their night time adventures.

Everything in Newport appeared to be perfectly normal. Peter and Sarah wandered off in order to purchase sweets, while Aunt Myf raided the supermarket. They were waiting outside the store for their Aunt to finish her BIG SHOP, when Peter had another surprise.

A large, broken-down caravan was parked nearby. The decrepit motor vehicle that was supposed to pull it had a flat tyre. A man was underneath, trying to get the wheel off. Unfortunately for him, one of the local police had chosen that moment to inspect his road tax licence. A heated exchange ensued. Then the man came out from under the car and Peter saw that it was...

"Kevin! What on earth is he doing here?" Peter pushed Sarah round a corner and stood close beside her so that Kevin might not recognise them.

"Is that the guy who saw the beast?" asked Sarah, for she had not actually noticed him on that day at Lands End.

"It's him, alright. What is he doing here, though?"

From the windows of the caravan, the rest of Kevin's family peered out.

"They couldn't be following the beast, could they?" Sarah said incredulously.

"I don't know, Sis, they might. I'm sure these Sympathetic Earthers are quite barmy enough."

"Shouldn't we warn them?"

"Not just now I don't think."

The exchange was becoming louder.

"I don't think that we want to get mixed up in any of that. Come on, let's go and find Catrin and Aunty."

An hour later they were back home, just in time to see Uncle Tomos off back to his work.

"We're sure to catch them tonight!" he said, looking confident for once. "We nearly had 'em last night, but they slipped through our fingers. My sergeant Pugh swore he actually saw them."

As Uncle Tomos said this, Peter and Sarah looked at each other but said nothing. What had Sergeant Pugh seen? What if it was them? Peter wondered if he should tell Uncle Tomos about Kevin. However, he thought better of it as on reflection, it might only complicate matters. Anyway, that nice policeman in Newport might have put Kevin into custody, with a bit of luck!

Uncle Tomos bade everyone goodbye and went away, saying:

"We'll bag 'em tonight, you see if we don't!"

"I hope you do, dear," said Aunt Myf, as she shut the front door. Then she turned to Peter and Sarah.

"Rather, I hope that Gwyn and Ederyn succeed and we see the last of that THING tonight. When you go, please be extra careful. Your Mother and Father return on Saturday. I don't want to have to return you to them as ashes and dust! It is all getting far too dangerous. If there is to be another night of this, I might not let you go."

"But we must know how it all ends," cried Peter.

He was fearful that, as yet, he had not been able to help the Elves with their small problem. Not doing so might mean that he failed *The Test* again, or at most, scraped a pass with poor marks.

"Please, dear Aunty," Sarah said with her sweetest smile.

"You may go tonight, but after that, I make no promises."

Aunt Myf folded her arms and went back into the kitchen where Catrin was 'helping' her to make rock cakes.

The third night followed the same pattern as before, except that this time Anir and the rest of the group arrived even earlier. Half past eleven the knock was heard at the front door. There was the usual exchange between Anir and Aunt Myf about being careful. Peter and Sarah climbed on to the two spare horses and they were off again, this time straight to the Prescelly Mountains just about as fast as you can go with horses on metalled roads. When they arrived at Tafarny Bwlch and began to climb up to Foel Cwm Cerwyn, Anir halted them all for a brief time. As he drew aside his cloak to reach for something, Peter noticed that Anir was fully armed. His great sword swung from his belt and a shield was slung over his horses side. He brought out from a saddle bag two small knives for Peter and Sarah:

"Just in case," as he said.

Although what use a knife (or short sword as they were in Sarah's eyes) would be against the Troynt is doubtful. Certainly, Sarah thought to herself, it would be rather like trying to kill a thunder cloud with a sewing needle. However, Anir seemed to think that it might afford some protection and it would look ungrateful to refuse, so she took it.

As usual, Sarah could see that Peter was delighted to be included in the band of Elvish warriors. The Lady Aneryn had once again come as Eirwen's chaperone. The Elf maid's presence seemed to make Peter want to show off. He suddenly urged his horse on, cantering past the three Watchers, so that he was level with Anir, who was leading.

"Show off!" thought Sarah, "and not even with the pretence of asking Anir any more of his daft questions!" and she lined her own mount up with that of Aneryn who rode behind Eirwen.

They took up their positions in almost exactly the same place as the first night. A dim glow spread from fires already lit to the north. The waning moon cast its pale light on the cairn at Prescelly Top. Mists rose out of the Old Quarry below them.

Sarah shuddered. It might look like an old quarry, but it was also the dark entrance to the underground realm that had once been presided over by Arddu. She often asked herself how many of his evil creatures could have survived that last battle with their dark and evil master. Might they awake, she wondered if the beast should call on them for assistance. She looked at Eirwen, who did not appear to be enjoying herself overmuch either.

"Now it's come to the point," Sarah said to herself, "I bet she's just as scared as I am!"

Then for the umpteenth time, Sarah muttered under her breath:

"Why, oh why am I here again?"

Though deep down she had to admit that she knew why. There was something, oh so very attractive about the Elves. She glanced sideways at Aneryn, whom she thought to be the most beautiful person that she had ever met.

"Beauty inside," Sarah thought, "as well as outside."

The Watchers also, the moonlight shining on their armour and in their golden hair gave them an ethereal quality. As they sat motionless on their white steeds, they almost seemed to float above the earth.

Then too, there was her barmy brother who seemed more and more determined to get as close to the Elves as possible. Well, just let him try! See if she cared! He was certainly into all this battle THING.

"I suppose I'll have to keep an eye on him," Sarah said with sisterly feeling, "someone with some common sense must... and it looks as if there's no-one else around, so it better be me."

A strange noise brought Sarah back to reality. There was a rustling beneath them in the valley below. Very quietly, about five hundred Elves with bows and arrows came up behind them. They were led by Ederyn. Anir gave him a kind of salute and Ederyn rode up beside him to give him the latest information and orders. Peter sat bolt upright on his horse, straining to hear what passed between them. Ederyn spoke in a low whisper:

"Gwyn is coming down from Crymych," was all the news that Peter managed to glean.

It was a little after midnight. Flames showed on the road in the valley, but they were not from the Troynt. They were from torches held aloft by another Legion of Elves. They were passing through Mynachlogddu. It was Gwyn-ap-Nudd.

"That THING can't be far away now," Peter thought, as he felt tingles of excitement play up and down his spine.

He was correct. Shortly after this, they all heard a great noise, over and behind the Prescelly Mountains. It was coming from a small village called Elwyswrw. Then they heard sirens once more: police cars, fire engines, ambulances, and then another, different sound.

"OH my goodness!" exclaimed Sarah to Eirwen, "they've got a helicopter out!"

"What is that?"

"I'll explain later. Hey, is that Anir on the move?"

Anir was moving his group to one side to let the Elvish army through. They went as quickly as Peter and Sarah had seen anything move. Swiftly they passed across the peaks.

"Where are they going?" Peter asked Anir.

"They are going to find the track that will lead them down to Gorse Fawr,"

"How do they know that IT will come?"

"They know! Look, Gwyn is at the other side already. It is time we went down also."

"Why?"

"Do you hear that roar?"

"Yes."

"Well, Peter, that is the beast on its way to light a bonfire on the top of these cairns. We had better not be too near when it does!" Anir dismounted.

The others in his party did the same and led their horses for a while down the tracks. Sarah did not like this route at all. It was far too near the Old Quarry. When the road was reached, they all mounted up once more and trotted away towards the Stone Circle at Gorse Fawr. Sarah wondered what the time was. The night wore on. It was in fact nearly two o'clock.

Anir's group came through a place where there were some trees and then they crossed a river. Another track brought them out by some farm buildings. They hid in the shadows by one of these and waited. Peter was so excited, he thought he would burst!

The Elvish army was gathering. One half to their right, coming down the road; the other to their left. Maniple upon maniple came ever onwards, and legion upon legion of Elves; swords and spears rustling and gleaming in the moonlight..

"Who is chasing the Troynt down to the Circle?" Peter asked Anir.

"Look, and you will see!" the grim Guardian answered, pointing upwards to the mountains above.

A noise as of ten fighter jet engines, roaring and screaming, came down from the heights. The Cairns became ringed with fire. Above and around, the flames and shadows cast by the Troynt were yet another maniple of Elf warriors, goading the beast onwards and downwards to the Stone Circle, but at the same time, towards those whose orders were to be *onlookers only*!

CHAPTER NINE

The Troynt Is Dismissed!

In their state of high excitement, or was it fright? None of the children, man, or Elf noticed a caravan parked in the farmer's yard that lay not all that far away from the Stone Circle where Gwyn-ap-Nudd intended to rid himself of the beast. Equally, the occupants of the caravan had no idea of what was going outside.

They were all sound asleep. 'They' being Kevin and his young family. They had actually come to Wales for some peace and quiet, their activities being entirely unconnected with the movements of the Troynt. Kevin had indeed been persuaded to visit the Police Station and was almost arrested for assaulting an officer. However, Detective Sergeant Montgomery Pugh, (Monty to his friends) had seen fit to let him off with a caution, after he promised to buy a license for his car immediately.

Now Kevin and his family lay unwittingly in the most dangerous of places; right in the path of the Troynt, who was by this time gaining in strength and very angry!

The Elves were intent on the business in hand. This night they were having a much better time of it and were well on the way to gaining the upper hand. The fire spitting beast had been driven from its hideout by the arrows and blades of the Elves, and a certain recipe that was known only to the Immortals. The Troynt roared as it passed over the tops and Cairns of the Prescelly Mountain range. It came almost directly, in a straight line from Eglwyswrw.

Past various hamlets and farms it came, but fortunately for them it was in too much of a hurry to attack. Then it rushed on, straight over Carnalaw, then across the Roman road, past Carn Arthur and down the gully towards the Standing Stones at Mon. It was approaching them across a small road with a noise like fifty steam locomotives, and certainly with as much fire in its belly. The Elves behind it kept going. The other two parts of the army drew together in a pincer movement, to cut off its progress beyond the Gorse Fawr Stone Circle.

"It would have to be such a small circle too," Sarah fretted.

The ring of stones was nowhere near the size of the Circle in Cornwall. Would it work? With the imminent arrival of the fiend, Sarah hoped very much that it would! She looked at Peter and Eirwen. They sat motionless but attentive on their horses, a little behind the Watchers and Anir, as if they were waiting for further orders.

A bright light sprang from the band of Elves to their right. Gwyn-ap-Nudd rode up to the Gorse Fawr Circle. In his hand he held aloft the Stone of Gardar. Great beams of light shone out from it. Peter felt that he could explode with the strain of waiting. Soon, he knew, Gwyn would utter the secret words, older than Time, which opened the portal in the Stone. Then the beast would be gone and everything would be alright again. He listened to the not so distant sound of many, many sirens. All the police cars, ambulances and fire engines in Wales seemed to bearing down on them. Gwyn had better hurry with his plan.

The Watchers suddenly dismounted and ran forwards to the Stones. Each one placing himself by one of the megaliths.

"Ah, ha!" thought Peter, "so that's THEIR job, I see."

Anir looked at the rest of his group.

"Any volunteers?" he asked.

Eirwen leapt forward straight away without thinking.

"I'll go," she said, and ran to one of the Stones.

"She would do that, wouldn't she," thought Sarah.

Peter's heart jumped into his mouth. He thought immediately that this stone-hugging must be going to form part of his testing. At once he readied himself to join Eirwen.

Sarah looked at Peter. He was obviously going to volunteer. Good, then she would not have to. Childkind would have a representative, but it would not have to be Sarah Jones!

The beast was almost upon them now, there was not much time for deliberation. Peter was on the point of dismounting, when something took his eye that he instantly knew was not right. At once Peter leaped back into the saddle, urged his horse to a trot and then a canter and a gallop. On he went as swiftly as he knew how, towards something that the beastly Troynt had set ablaze on its way to the Stones.

Sarah felt almost like fainting again. She could not think what might have possessed Peter to gallop off in such a fashion. If Anir knew, he did not say. All that he did say was to ask for another volunteer to go to the Stones. Everyone looked at Sarah. With a sinking feeling, she knew they were all expecting *her* to go. She hesitated just for a second, there was no time to lose! Most reluctantly, Sarah jumped down from her horse and joined the others by a stone, feeling rather like the ugly duckling among the swans. A brick in her stomach and her head swimming, Sarah put her hand on the stone in front of her.

Meanwhile, what had Peter seen that was so urgent that it required his immediate attention? It was only an old car burning after all. But the flames thrown up by the burning automobile displayed, darkly against them, the shape of an equally old caravan. Peter instinctively knew that it was Kevin's! Having seen the family with their dilapidated transport only a few hours ago, it was easily recognisable. Doubtless, Kevin and his poor little family were asleep inside it, knowing nothing of the conflagration and raging battle outside. Peter took no thought as to the danger he was in.

"If that car explodes..." he thought, "it'll take out the caravan and the people inside it. I have to get them out of there before it goes up!"

Peter reined in his horse until it stood beside the caravan. Elvish horses are fearless and trained to display the highest discipline in all circumstances. Peter leapt from its back and banged on the door, again and again with all his might. There was no response. Suppose they were overcome by fumes from the burning vehicle? Peter tried again to rouse the family. Then he lost patience and tried to force the door. No good, he was not strong enough. He must think and not panic.

"The horse, use the horse!" he told himself at last.

It could kick the door in. Peter leapt back on the horse and made it walk backwards to the caravan door.

"Please kick it in," he cried desperately, hoping it would understand him.

Obediently, the Elf horse edged back, gave a buck and kicked out with its hind legs. Its hooves smacked on to the door and thank goodness, the door gave way. Peter dismounted once more. The smell of burning oil was heavy in the air as Peter ran into the caravan to rouse the sleeping occupants.

"Fire! Fire!" Peter yelled as loudly as he could.

The family proved lethargic and difficult to rouse. Perhaps they had indeed suffered from inhaling noxious gases from their car, which was by this time almost completely incinerated. Hardly knowing what he was doing, Peter ran into the caravan and grabbed one of Kevin's tiny children. This made the mother move. She shot out after him, clutching the other little one to her breast and Kevin followed.

"Get away from here, quick!" Peter shouted at the bewildered family.

Their temporary home had now caught fire also. Peter pushed them all over to one of the nearby farm buildings, one that was fortunately built of stone. They ran quickly behind the wall of the old building. The toddlers began to cry, then too, their mother.

"There, there," Kevin said, patting her on the shoulder, "we're all safe. That's wot counts!"

They had been rescued not a moment too soon. With a loud report, the car exploded in flames and shortly afterwards, the gas canisters in the caravan did the same.

"Boo, hoo, hoo!" went Kevin's family.

"That settles it, Marina, we're going to get a proper home next time!" Kevin said emphatically, as he watched the remains of their past life imitate a funeral pyre. "A proper home!" he repeated.

Then he looked at Peter.

"Thanks, young man," he said, "you've saved our lives. Thank you very much."

Kevin then shook Peter warmly by the hand, making him feel very embarrassed and rather sorry that he had been so scathing about the Sympathetic Earthers.

At that moment, they were joined by Aneryn. At first Peter was surprised that Kevin, Marina and their children could see her. Then he remembered that although Elves cannot usually be seen by humankind, they may be seen if they themselves *wish* to be visible.

Aneryn went to work straightaway. There was a stool in the corner of the barn, or shed, or whatever it was they were in, and she made Marina sit on it. Then she wrapped her cloak round Marina and the smaller of the two children, made Kevin sit down on some old hay beside her, and put the other child in his arms. Then Aneryn produced a silver bottle and a cup. She poured some liquid into the cup and made each member of Kevin's family drink it. After that, they seemed to cheer up a bit.

"I will wait here with these people until the rescue teams arrive," Aneryn said to Peter, after he too had had some of the drink. "That was a very brave thing you just did, Peter, and the Lord Gwyn shall know of it directly. But for now, you might care to go and see how your sister and the others are faring!"

Peter suddenly thought of what might be happening at the Stone Circle.

"Thanks Aneryn, I'll go and see at once."

Peter drew his short sword and led the horse quietly back to where he could see what was going on.

Sarah had gone to stand by a stone with the others, albeit unwillingly. The others were all Elves. Why did they want her? She had not the slightest idea of how to release the secret forces pent up in these weirdly hewn stones. Then she looked at Eirwen.

144

"I bet she doesn't know either," Sarah said under her breath.

Eirwen was already holding on to her stone with her eyes tight shut. If Sarah had been able to enquire of the Elf maid, she would have discovered that Eirwen was *absolutely terrified*. Eirwen now thought that this present adventure was no fun at all. In fact she was wishing that she could be back in Arx Emain with nice Aunty Morvith and washing cups up in the Babies' Nursery.

"The beast comes! The beast comes! Hold the Stones!" shouted the Lord Gwyn above the noise of the furious, angry, beastly Troynt.

The noise from the Sirens was also beginning to be overpowering and obviously extremely close.

"They must have reached Crymych by now," Sarah thought, "I do hope this will all be over soon. It would be too awful to get arrested by one's Uncle, or even by his Detective Sergeant!"

She touched the Stone in front of her. A most curious tingle ran up and down the whole of her body.

"Odd," she thought, "most odd."

Sarah looked at Eirwen, who was clearly frightened to death, but refusing to admit it.

"Well, if it's OK for her to be scared, then it's OK for me," Sarah said to herself.

Then she too clung to her Stone with eyes tight shut, so that she might not see the dreadful beast and fail in her duty.

The Troynt came on apace. It was almost at the Stones. Peter came through the lines of the Elvish infantry and then watched from behind his horse. He saw how frightened Sarah must be and was sorry that it had to be Sarah and not himself that stood at the Stones. Still, it was too late now, much too late.

The Elvish army stood, arrows, swords and spears at the ready, their bows bending, their shields up. Finally, like a gale, the Troynt was upon them and in the Stone Circle.

"NOW!" cried Gwyn-ap-Nudd.

The Stone handlers hugged their Stones. Sarah was shocked to find that the tingling sensation she had experienced before increased, until really it was beginning to be unpleasant. If she had looked, she would have seen what Peter saw. The Troynt was writhing in fury, or perhaps it might have been pain. Peter could not tell. It was still powerful enough to spit fire and quite a few of Gwyn's army were badly burnt.

The horrible fiend did not seem to want to be un-empowered. It fought against the power of the Elves and the Stones up to the last minute. Peter gave his horse's reins to one of the Elves standing by. Something in his bones told him that Sarah and Eirwen were in deadly danger and should not have been there.

"That Eirwen! She's either very brave or completely stupid," Peter said to himself, as he crept closer and closer to the Stone Circle.

Unnoticed, Anir followed him with the same thought in mind, until they were both standing behind one of the girls. At that precise moment, the Troynt gasped its last gasp and gave up. But not without spinning round the Circle to give its enemies one last blast of fire. Of course, those who had their eyes open could avoid the flames, but Sarah and Eirwen still had theirs shut. There was no way that they could take any precautions.

"It was almost like dragon's breath!" Ederyn said later, when they were discussing the day's adventure at Arx Emain.

Peter could see at once that Eirwen was in danger of catching the full force of the blast. Without hesitation, Peter made his best Rugger tackle ever! He managed to pull her down and out of reach of the fire. Anir did much the same with Sarah. The Watchers had all ducked down immediately.

The Troynt cried out with a most fearful and wretched cry. Gwyn-ap-Nudd opened the portal in the Gardar Stone. Then he uttered strange words that seemed to come from another place, almost as if from the depths of the earth. The frightful fiend began to fade. Its shape wobbled and went thinner and flatter, until finally, it passed through the magic portal and out of sight.

A great cry went up from all the assembled Elves. Their final night's exercises had been successful and the Troynt was gone, hopefully for ever.

The Lord Gwyn closed the portal. When the Stone of Gardar had shrunk to its normal size, he placed it in the bag which was slung on a belt at his waist and made ready to leave at the head of his troops. He gave a wink to Ederyn, which Peter noticed and took to mean:

"No losing it THIS time!"

The children had all clung to each other until it was all over. Then Ederyn began to march his part of the army away. The Watchers went away with those who had come down the mountain behind the beast. Before he went, Ederyn leant forward from his horse and spoke to Peter and Sarah.

"No time for many words now, dear friends, for I have my duties. Though I promise you there shall be time later, when we are all back at Arx Emain. We will make time, for you have both done *very well indeed*. Our gracious thanks to you for all that you have done for us tonight. We shall meet again soon and thank you properly, I hope! Farewell, Peter, Sarah."

"Farewell, Ederyn!" they cried, waving to him as he left at the head of his troops.

Eirwen was placed up on the saddle behind him. Peter nudged Sarah in the ribs:

"He's not taking any more chances with her! I bet she's not allowed to go far outside Arx Emain after this."

"I expect she's had all the fun she can take, for the present at least. I know I have," Sarah said, "but where did you get to? What happened, where did you gallop off to in such a hurry?" Peter suddenly remembered Kevin and his family.

"Oh, my goodness! Where's Anir? Aneryn must still be with them."

Peter ran off straightaway, but this time with Sarah close on his heels. As a matter of fact, Anir was already making his way to where Aneryn was taking care of the burnt out Sympathetic Earthers. Kevin had wandered out of the barn to get some fresh air and had unfortunately witnessed the *goings-on* at the Stone Circle. The process of taming the Troynt had made him even more determined to find a more normal way of life for his family, and so he put his mind to the problem at once.

Aneryn comforted Marina and the children as best she could, until the fire brigade arrived with the police and ambulance not far behind. Kevin explained everything to the Police, though Detective Sergeant Montgomery Pugh could not make much sense out of the story. When Peter appeared at the door with Anir and Sarah, the whole family hailed him as their hero. At last, the Firemen grasped what had occurred, the chief said that Peter deserved a medal. Sarah felt immensely proud to have a brother who was so brave.

"I never thought about it," Peter said, and just shrugged his shoulders. "I only did what had to be done, Sarah was brave too," he told them.

"I saw what happened," he told her, when none of the others were listening, "you were tremendous."

Then the Police said that Peter should have an award, or a commendation. The paramedics agreed, as a terrible tragedy had been averted and they had only had to treat minor burns.

"We'd rather do that than see third degree burns," they said. They also thanked Aneryn for her valuable assistance.

"You must have gone to an excellent first-aid course," they told her, as they congratulated her on her treatment for shock.

By the time that Uncle Tomos arrived, or Detective Inspector Davies, as he was when he was on duty, everyone THOUGHT they knew what had happened. Uncle Tomos was ever so slightly surprised, it has to be said, when he found Peter and Sarah out on the other side of the Prescelly mountains in the middle of the night. Although, by this time, it was the early hours of the morning.

Peter thought quickly and said that they had come out with friends to have a look at the wild life of the Prescelly Mountains at night. This of course was partially true, the wild life that they had gone to view being the Troynt, of course! And it had been very WILD!

"We just got carried away," said Peter, "it was all so absorbing, and then we found these poor people about to be fried, so we went to help."

This sounded quite a reasonable excuse, all in all, and Uncle Tomos was inclined to let it go at that. Then too, every one who had been involved with the rescue of Kevin, Marina and their children agreed that Peter was the hero of the hour.

Sarah and Peter went home in the fire engine for a treat. Kevin and his family were taken to the local hospital for treatment and rest. Uncle Tomos went with Detective Sergeant Montgomery Pugh to the Constabulary to try and sort out the night's events. The whole Police Force was entirely mystified and *The Case of the Phantom Arsonist* remained forever open.

When Uncle Tomos came home the next day for lunch, he wanted Aunt Myf to explain how it was that Peter and Sarah had been out all night. Naturally, Peter had primed her and she was able to follow the same story, with a slight addition:

"Peter and Sarah went out to see wild life with my distant cousin, Anir and his wife, Aneryn. They are both dedicated environmentalists, very keen on wild nature and all that sort of thing, they are, and I thought it would be a nice holiday treat for Peter and Sarah to go up on the hills at night.

Of course I would have gone myself, but Catrin's having trouble with a tooth again. Oh yes, I would trust Anir with my life! He looks a bit rough because he works out in the open all the time. He is a sort of warden for the countryside and is a real gem. You must meet him sometime."

"With pleasure, Myfanwy,"

"Oh dear, there goes Catrin again. Do you want to take the tooth gel up to her, or shall I?"

Uncle Tomos went upstairs to Catrin with good grace. When he had gone out of hearing, Peter said:

"You told him about Anir!"

"And why shouldn't I? He is a cousin when all's said and done and I believe it is always better to tell the truth and shame the Devil. Also, my darlings It is better that husbands and wives should have no secrets between them. You might remember that when you get older. Anyway, the rate you two have adventures, my poor Tomos will have to meet Anir sooner or later, I'm sure he will."

For most of the morning, Peter and Sarah had been asleep and it was not until they woke up that they told Aunt Myf everything that had happened during the fateful night. Aunt Myf was very pleased with them both, especially about the rescue. The rest of that day they spent quietly, but the next day began with a letter from the Chief Constable, inviting Peter and Sarah to receive a medal. Somehow, Sarah had become caught up in the general celebrations and indeed, she fully deserved a share in the honours. All that anyone cared about was the fact that the fire raising had ceased.

There was a grand ceremony at the Town Hall, with all sorts of dignitaries present. There were officers from the Fire Brigade and people from the Ambulance Service. A speech was made and the medals given out. Pictures were taken for the papers and there was even a man from the Television station. Uncle Tomos basked in their reflected glory, together with his Detective Sergeant. Aunt Myf then treated everyone to tea at a café in Town. Peter and Sarah felt quite overwhelmed.

Next day, everything returned to a sort of normality. Uncle Tomos went to work at the usual time and Peter and Sarah settled down to enjoy the rest of their last day with Aunt Myf before Mother and Father were due to come home. But then, at half past ten, there was a familiar knock on the door, and there stood Anir once again.

"The Lord Gwyn desires your presence at a celebration," he said, smiling at the two children. Aunt Myf had them all ready to go out before you could turn round, even Catrin.

"I was going to go to the shops in Haverfordwest today or tomorrow anyway," she said. "I'll give you all a lift to Arx Emain, there and back if you like!"

She was as good as her word. Anir came too, of course. The three children in the back seats had once again to suffer another non-stop discussion and dissection of family life according to Clan Jones!

"Why do grown-ups always do that?" Peter asked himself, yet again.

They arrived at Arx Emain promptly at twelve, just in time for the Elves' midday meal. This time Peter and Sarah could see that it was to be a very splendid affair. Silver and gold cloth mixed with the more normal blues, reds, greens and greys of the Elves' dress.

The procession of food into the Great Hall of Gwyn-ap-Nudd was grand beyond description. Peter and Sarah sat with Eirwen on either side of Anir, Aneryn, Ederyn and Gwyn upon the High Table. A hearty meal was had by all. Then, when the last toast had been drunk to the dregs, Gwyn-ap-Nudd called for silence.

Peter and Sarah were made to stand before the Elf King while he made speeches all about them. How Peter had not only saved the lives of the human travellers, but he had saved the life of Eirwen also. His courage was not in question and he had shown that he was definitely made of the stuff of heroes. He was then asked to kneel and receive a golden medallion containing a small green stone. Peter felt most embarrassed and blushed a nice deep crimson. As the Elf King placed the chain around Peter's neck he whispered something:

"Congratulations!" he said, "you did not fail us this time. I knew you would not. That is another trial over with. Well done, you are truly *on the way* now!"

This Peter knew referred to the Tests for the Guardianship, or was it for the Apprenticeship for the Guardianship? At this moment Peter did not care. He could not have been happier, now that he knew he had won through, hopefully to the next stage... whatever that might turn out to be.

Then it was Sarah's turn. Without her, Gwyn said, the circle of the power of the Stones would have been incomplete. She had faced the terror of the Troynt with much bravery and had not flinched from her duty. Great waves of applause ensued. Sarah also knelt to receive a medallion. Then even more applause accompanied Peter and Sarah back to their seats.

The ceremony was now over. Gwyn and Ederyn with their entourage left the Hall in magnificent procession. Anir, Aneryn and Eirwen then took Peter and Sarah to where Morvith was looking after Dylan again. They sat quietly in Morvith's room, talking of everything in general and nothing in particular, until it was time for Peter and Sarah to leave. All said farewell to each other except for Anir, who was to guide Peter and Sarah back to the main road in order to meet up with their Aunt.

"I am sure we will see you again soon," said Aneryn and Morvith.

"I do hope I see you again soon," said Eirwen.

Then Anir led Peter and Sarah away. They made a brief visit to the Room of the Stone, just to see if it had really and truly come back to its niche in one piece!

Then, on their way to the front door of Arx Emain, Anir stopped in the Outer Hall and made the two children a speech of gratitude.

"You have done exceptionally well, both of you. Even though you were frightened, Sarah, you did what you knew was necessary when your brother was called away to other things. That is true heroism. To go through with something even though you are scared. It was, as you rightly guessed, essential to the Power of the Stones that one of the operative members of the Circle should be a Human! I was, as it were, there for other purposes and could not go. When Peter flew off, it left you alone to fill his place and destiny. Now the Troynt is gone and we are all extremely grateful to you, as the Lord Gwyn said earlier."

He patted Sarah on the back appreciatively. Then turning to Peter, Anir smiled and beamed at him with the greatest satisfaction:

"Now I come to you, Peter," he said, "I have to tell you that you most certainly passed **The Test** this time! You acted with great initiative to rescue not only Kevin and Company, but our lovely Eirwen also. The Lord Gwyn and Eirwen's own family will be for ever grateful to you for that."

Then Anir looked deep into Peter's eyes.

"Yes," he said, "this time you *did* pass **The Test** and excellently so! Speaking personally, I am very pleased, very pleased indeed. If I am a good judge of character, I think you will pass through them *all*. I thought that you would see through Gwyn's little ruse to try and put you off joining the chase and so you did; thus achieving even greater things than Gwyn himself foresaw. It is well, very well. I shall look forward to seeing what you do with the next trial! May the Power of All Powers ever be with you."

The sound of horses hooves on the stone floor outside the Outer Hall announced their departure. Peter and Sarah were hurried out by Anir and were soon mounted and riding out over the spring countryside to meet their Aunt.

No sooner had they patted their horses and said goodbye to Anir, than Aunt Myf arrived in her car. It was evident from Catrin's appearance that their Aunt had indulged herself in the Baby Shop and bought some very pretty little things for the toddler.

They returned to the house in Newport in time for supper. Peter and Sarah were glad that evening to have an early night. Tomorrow they would have to pack and get ready for Father and Mother's return.

"Quite some holiday it's been," said Sarah, as they were on the point of falling asleep.

"Quite a time, Sis, but I wouldn't have missed it for anything. It will be a nice rest to go back to school! There's just one thing, though,"

"What's that?"

"We ought to have written to Emma and Amy. They'll be simply furious that they've missed it all!"

"Never mind, we'll phone them in the morning. Now goodnight Peter, I'm going to sleep."

"Goodnight, Sis," said Peter.

Then there was silence while Sarah passed into the land of dreams. Peter joined her there a little later, but not before he had pondered over Anir's parting words to him. The words of praise he had received from The Guardian were worth more than all the medals to Peter. He had passed The Test, and well, too! This must mean that he was safely on the way to becoming apprenticed to Anir, and that meant everything to Peter.

"To be Apprentice Guardian," he thought, "and some day perhaps, to be The Guardian himself... what more could anyone want?"

Sarah awoke to find the sun shining brightly on her bedcover and Peter standing at the open window.

"It's a beautiful day. Do hurry and get up Sarah, it's late and we've got to pack after breakfast."

Mother and Father were due back home after lunch, which meant there was not much time in which to get things ready for school on the following day. Although they still felt tired from all their nightly exertions, the morning had to be spent in a flurry of activity. Aunt Myf had prepared an early lunch so that her niece and nephew would be ready to leave when their parents arrived.

At twelve fifteen, the first course was over and a most splendid apple pie of vast proportions was just opened, when there were several loud knocks at the front door. Uncle Tomos went to see who it was. It was, of course, Dr. and Mrs. Jones! After ecstatic and enthusiastic greetings all round, Mother and Father, complete with souvenirs and presents for everyone, were ushered into the dining room.

"Here, have some apple pie, Mum, it's really great," said Peter.

"Well, I rather think I will. We've had a long drive. What about you, John?"

"Yes indeed! I can't resist your sister's pies."

Then came the exchange of gifts and news. Peter and Sarah wanted to hear all about Granada, but first came the news of Peter and Sarah's heroic deeds, with all the medals, certificates and newspaper cuttings as proof! Mother did not say much, but you could tell that she was very pleased. Father said that he was very glad that his children could be trusted to keep their heads in a tricky situation and that they were reliable and responsible children. Then he gave them two pounds each.

"I am afraid that is all I have left. But I promise that you will have a special treat next weekend, the cinema perhaps?"

"Cool!" said Peter and Sarah at once.

Mother and Father stayed and talked until nearly tea time. Then finally, they said they MUST go and leave Aunt Myf, Uncle Tomos and Catrin to some peace and quiet.

Peter and Sarah thanked Aunt Myf energetically for having them to stay, then picked up their bags and followed Mother and Father out of the house.

"Goodbye and thank you!" they called, and were soon on the way home, to their cottage by the sea.

Over a late supper, Mother and Father showed Peter and Sarah all the photographs they had taken. Then they told them an extra piece of news that was a surprise to the children, but not totally unexpected.

"We're thinking of having Grandmother to live with us here. What do you think of THAT?" said Father, shutting the last photo album with a bang.

"Gosh," said Sarah, "is she ill?"

"Not ill as such," Mother told her, "but she is over eighty now and rather frail since that last bout of pneumonia."

"Where will she live?" asked Peter.

"In Briar Cottage, of course!" answered Father.

"But it's full of all our old junk."

"Yes," said Mother, "It is now, but we can soon clear it up. I know it's only two rooms, well, three with the bathroom, but I think if it's redecorated it will do. After all, the people who had this cottage before Aunt Myf used to farm Tourists in there once upon a time!"

"Yes," said Sarah, "We know."

She had heard the history of the old cow byre at the end of their garden, many, many times! She now rehearsed it again for the benefit, or not, of all present!

"And before the Tourists, cows lived in it and the Farmer used to call it Byre Cottage, but the Tourists preferred Briar Cottage, and that's what stuck!"

"Well, I think it's a jolly good idea," said Peter.

"And it will be such fun to make it look all nice for Gran," Sarah agreed.

"It will," said Father, "but first, I rather think we had better have a car-boot sale!" everyone laughed. It was all settled.

Later that evening, Peter remembered that they had forgotten to telephone Emma and Amy, so they did it straight away, before there was time to forget again.

"We thought you'd died!" was Emma's first comment, but she was eager to hear all about the defeat of the Beastly Troynt nevertheless.

"It's safely buried under a huge mound in Ireland," said Sarah, "and it will never get out again."

"Are you quite sure?" Amy asked, when she was allowed to speak.

"Quite," Peter and Sarah told her very firmly, knowing what Amy was like!

They chatted on, telling the girls everything. Then they wished them luck in the Summer Term. But, before they rang off Emma told Sarah that she had forgotten something important when she left Falmouth. Sarah could not immediately think what that could be. Gleefully, Emma reminded her:

"The Cards! You left us your Bugglitz cards!"

Sarah had completely forgotten all about such things in the excitement of her recent adventures, and told Emma that Amy could have them all. Amy was thrilled.

"Perhaps we'll meet again in the next Hols," Emma said hopefully.

"Hope so," said Sarah, but then Mother came and said they had chatted enough, and made signs for them to ring off.

So, the Easter Holidays and their adventures were both at an end, but there was one more surprise to come. On the following Saturday, a large parcel arrived for Peter and Sarah. It was a big box wrapped up in brown paper and tied up with string. When it was unwrapped, it revealed a massive glass dish with Peter and Sarah's names engraved upon it, and the words:

"Thanks, from Kevin, Marina, Kaytie and Adam."

There was a letter too, in which Peter was thanked over and over again for saving them all from a dreadful fiery fate. There was also an explanation of the dish.

"We ain't got much no more, but we got this dish and Marina's friend does glass work and etching and such, up in Cardigan. We hope you like it. Kevin thinks he will go and work at the glass works now, as it looks like an interesting job. Our thanks again."

"How very nice of them," said Mother, "I'm sure you deserve it."

"I am sure they do," Father concurred, "perhaps one day we'll go and visit the glass works and see how Kevin is getting on, I much admire people who blow glass. Of course, in the Roman times..." but at the mention of *Romans*, Peter and Sarah jumped on him in an attempt to dissuade him from giving them a lecture on ancient history.

Later, as the two children got ready for bed, they reflected on their extraordinary holiday.

"I do hope Kevin and his family will be alright now," said Sarah.

"I expect so, though I don't think they'll want to be Sympathetic Earthers again in a hurry."

"I suppose not."

"There is just one thing I'd like to know, though, Sis,"

"And what, my dear brother, is that?"

"How many of these Tests do I have to pass? And what will the next one be? When will it come? Anir mentioned them again when we left Arx Emain. And..."

"Oh no!" said Sarah, "Not again! You can ask him yourself the next time we see him, and I hope that will be soon because we shall not have any peace until you get an answer!"

With that reply, Peter had to be content. But as Sarah remarked sometime later, he was often thinking about **The Tests** now, and was not above mentioning them, and quite frequently too. At last, Peter had divulged a very small part of his BIG secret to her. Sarah agreed not to TELL, and to give him her undying support. But what on earth might all these Tests be leading him to, she wondered?

After his awful time with the Shield of Agamemnon and the terrible mistake that he had made, Peter now knew. His act of disobedience against the Lord Gwyn had put his future with the Elves in jeopardy. Even though he knew that he was forgiven *all*, Peter had been extraordinarily anxious to make amends. At the time of his failure, The Lord Gwyn had told Peter quite clearly that any move forward towards the Guardianship depended on his full co-operation with any further trials. Thank goodness, he had come through this last one with full marks! He hoped it would make up for the one he had muffed.

"I wish I could spend more time at Arx Emain," Peter thought to himself, but it was no good; things like school and ordinary family life were always getting in the way. He could not just go off and stay there... not yet!

In a small way, this too was a Test and Peter was well aware of it. However, he was resolved to get through it all; whatever he felt about it and however long he might have to wait for the prize he was after.

Small wonder then, that he became more and more eager to receive the next challenge. Whatever it was, he would be ready for it. Peter had made up his mind about that and as Sarah would most likely tell you; Peter was noted for being stubborn! The more he had to do with Gwyn, Ederyn, Anir and all the citizens of Arx Emain, the more he wanted to join them and was ready to do anything to achieve this.

What that *anything* might be, Peter did not know and neither did he care; or at least he told himself that he did not, which is not quite the same thing. It was a sobering thought and one that Peter often contemplated in his quieter moments. For the present however, he told no-one else besides Sarah about it, preferring to keep his visions to himself.

And what of Eirwen? It seems that Eirwen had not passed 'The Test', or perhaps was not yet ready to take it. The next time that Peter and Sarah were in the company of the Elves of Arx Emain, they discovered that Eirwen had been sent home to her Mother and Father in the North Kingdom. Peter often wondered if he would ever see her again. Indeed, they were to meet anew, but not until the trees around the Kingdom of Gwyn-ap-Nudd had grown several measures taller and the snows had come and gone on the Cairns of Foel Cwm Cerwyn.

THE END